NIGHTWALKER 3

NIGHTWALKER 3
A POST-APOCALYPTIC WESTERN ADVENTURE

FRANK RODERUS

CRAIG MARTELLE

First US edition, May 2019
ISBN: 978-1-64202-213-1

CHAPTER ONE

The bad news was that he was an outlaw, wanted now by the Federal Command throughout the clear areas of what remained of the United States. The good news was that he was free—so far. Jim Wolfe walked cross-country through the rocks and canyons of the increasingly dry land along the border between Wyoming and Utah.

As far as he could determine, he had left the Wyoming clear area behind and was now in one of the red zones, where radiation contamination was too dangerous for human habitation. In truth, Wolfe would gladly have stayed in the safer clear area behind him, if it were not for the knowledge that he was, or very soon would be, declared an outlaw by the Federal Command.

After the exchange of nuclear weapons between the United States and the coalition of China, India, and North Korea, Wolfe hid for a couple years inside an abandoned mine tunnel. He stayed there until he ran out of the food that had been in the cargo he'd been carrying as a long-haul trucker. That, and the water that seeped like a mountain spring from the tunnel walls, sustained him.

When Wolfe finally emerged, both he and the world around him were drastically changed. He himself was unusually strong—perhaps due to radiation causing changes in the water, or possibly as the result of some chemical action—and his eyes no longer dilated normally. He could see perfectly well at night now, but during the day, was blinded by sunlight unless he wore the welding goggles that he'd found at an old service station. And, perhaps understandably, his hair had turned completely white.

Much more than the changes he found in himself, though, were the changes that had taken place in the country. State and local government had been abandoned in the declared clear areas. Governments fell to the hands of a single, Federal Command structure. While the military continued to fight a distant war, and America's enemies no longer had the means to deliver nuclear weapons to the North American continent, the Federal Command, commonly known as FEDCOM, granted citizens livelihood at little more than a subsistence level. Commodities were strictly rationed. Gasoline for private transportation was virtually nonexistent now, and luxury items like cigarettes and alcoholic beverages had disappeared from American life. Those contraband items could still be found, however, in the abandoned stores and warehouses inside the prescribed red zones, and a brisk trade had developed in them.

Scavengers who lived in the clear areas crossed into the red zones to find valuables and smuggle them past FEDCOM guards at the borders. It had been Jim Wolfe's bad luck to run afoul of a family of highly successful but vicious scavengers.

In the course of rescuing a friend of his from slavery at the hands of the Alston brothers, two of the Alstons had died. The surviving brothers, Ralph and Ed, undertook to pursue Wolfe. Their intent: to kill him to avenge the deaths they considered to have been murder. More recently, the Alstons themselves murdered several FEDCOM border guards and an elderly woman in the Wyoming clear area. They successfully blamed those murders on Wolfe, and now he was a fugitive from the FEDCOM inside the clear areas, and had a price on his head imposed by the Alstons in the red zones. That was the bad news.

The good, however, was that so far, he had eluded them. And, every day that passed, every foot of ground he covered, brought him that much closer to his home. Or, to where his home used to be.

With no long-distance communication, and virtually nothing in the way of news travelling from one clear area to another, he had no way to learn if Bradenton, Florida, still stood. After all, the little Gulf Coast town lay immediately south of Tampa Bay, where MacDill Air Force Base contained the military's Central Command. He had to assume that MacDill would have been targeted in the sequence of sneak attacks that destroyed so much of the country. MacDill was probably gone. But Wolfe continued to hold out hope that somehow, his wife, Lurleen, and their toddler son, Jojo, had survived.

Without them to go back to, he had little reason to go on, and he would not, he could not, rest until he got home and knew once and for all.

Trapped on the road in Idaho when the first bombs fell, Wolfe had a very long way to travel. Being an outlaw would not make that any easier for him, but then, neither that, nor anything else short of death, would stop him from getting back to Florida.

Wolfe opened a can of corned beef, gave half to the big German Shepherd mix dog that had become his traveling companion, and used a pair of twigs like chopsticks to eat his portion. It would soon be dark and he would be able to travel comfortably then.

"Maybe we've put our troubles behind us, boy. What do you think?" He scratched the dog behind its ears. Wolfe's hope that trouble was over and done with was only human—it was also very wrong.

CHAPTER TWO

Wolfe disliked walking inside the canyon. He felt cramped in there, restricted by the sandstone walls and the fact that he could not see far. His enemies could be close without him being aware of them, and that made him nervous. On the other hand, he had little real choice in the matter. He knew he could get along without food for weeks at a time if need be, but a human being absolutely must have water in order to sustain life. He could find water down in the bottoms, the low-lying areas even if he had to dig for it.

He stayed close to the canyon wall and paid attention to the dog as he walked. The dog was his early warning system. At least, he hoped it would warn him of danger. Of course, it was more apt to show him the presence of others by wagging its tail than by growling. The one time it had shown any aggression was back in Wyoming when it had attacked and badly slashed the face of Ed Alston. Wolfe figured that barely counted, since the dog was once owned by the Alstons and had been mistreated by them.

"What do you think, boy? It's getting close to daybreak.

Should we start looking for a place to hole up now?" Since resuming his journey, Wolfe's habit was to march during the night when he could see perfectly well and when he had less to fear from dehydration or heat, and hole up during the daylight hours. He also had decided to avoid the highways and paved roads now. There was no private vehicular traffic on them these days; the only motorized vehicles Wolfe had seen since he emerged from his refuge in the mine tunnel were a few—very few—FEDCOM trucks. Even so, he did not want to be out in the open along the highways. The easily-walked routes attracted scavengers, and as well were likely to be used by the wilders—the lawless few who seemed to enjoy the brutal anarchy that existed in the red zones—and by drifters who simply wanted to live free of the restrictions imposed by the government.

The problem with encountering strangers was that you never knew which sort of red zone dweller you had. Wolfe had run across some fine folks in the red zone up in Idaho. He'd also found himself involved with some of the other sort as well, and he did not want to take any chances—especially now that a price had been put on his head.

As the first pale hints of daylight began to lighten the upper rim of the canyon he'd been following, Wolfe looked for a side canyon or some niche where he could get out of the open. Nothing that he could see looked particularly inviting, and there seemed to be no water close, either. Still, the thought of travelling in this barren country during broad daylight was not at all appealing. He settled for making a nest of sorts behind a slab of rock that had fallen from the rim above, and pouring a scant cup full of water from one of the two canteens he carried. Little as it was, he shared it with the dog. Then, he pulled his dark goggles in place and laid down on top of the blankets that served him for a bed, his good sleeping bag and other possessions having been stolen by the Alston brothers a week or so back.

"Keep an eye on things while I'm sleeping, boy. Wake me if somebody comes," he said aloud, although, not with any expectation at all that the big dog would really do it.

CHAPTER THREE

It was just as well that Wolfe placed no great confidence in the dog. When he stirred and finally opened his eyes, he found himself looking at two young men, one of whom was petting the dog and grinning.

"Not much of a watch dog, is he?" that one asked.

The two were in their late teens or early twenties, Wolfe thought. Both wore grey sweatshirts, jeans, and sneakers. Both wore their hair in short buzz cuts and were clean shaven—a great rarity after the war when production of razor blades stopped and household electricity disappeared.

Wolfe sat up and stifled a yawn. "Who are you?"

The one by the dog said, "I'm Jason. My friend here is Leon." He stopped messing with the dog and asked, "And what is your business here?"

The question was ordinary enough, but Wolfe thought he could hear a slight edge in Jason's voice when he asked it. Wolfe introduced himself and then said, "I'm not here on any particular business. Just passing through on my way home."

"That would be…where?"

Wolfe told him.

"And you just happened to come this way?"

"That's right."

"Even though it would be shorter to cut east through the clear area over there?"

Wolfe shrugged.

"You really should answer the questions," Leon said.

Wolfe looked at him for a moment without saying anything. He snapped his fingers and the dog left Jason and came to Wolfe's side. Wolfe scratched the animal behind the ears.

"What's his name?" Jason asked.

"I haven't gotten around to giving him one. He travels with me. I feed him. I haven't thought of him as being my dog or anything."

"He looks like a wolf. Call him Lobo."

"Too obvious," Wolfe said. "Besides, then people would think I was talking about myself or something."

"Don't worry. I'll think of a good name for him," Jason said.

"It's a shame I won't be around to find out what it is. The dog and I will be moving along now."

"Not just yet," Leon said.

Wolfe hadn't been paying any particular attention until now, but it belatedly occurred to him that the rifle he'd placed beside his bedroll when he'd laid down to sleep was gone from that spot.

Jason and Leon were both armed, not that there was anything unusual about that here in the red zone, where virtually everyone went armed for sheer survival, but not with M16s like the FEDCOM troopers and Wolfe carried.

"Where's my rifle?"

"We didn't want you to misunderstand when you woke up. We're keeping it safe for you," Leon said.

"Fine. I'm awake now, and there's no misunderstanding. I'll have the rifle back now, if you please."

"Later."

"Now," Wolfe said calmly. If these youngsters thought they were going to intimidate him, they had a long way to go. Of course, because of the snow-white hair, they probably thought he was an old man. It was a common enough mistake. And they could have no way to know how quick and powerful he was. If he chose to hurt them, he could break both their necks before they had a chance to bring their lever-action rifles into play.

"Now," he said again.

Jason looked at his companion and nodded. "Give Mr. Wolfe back his gun, Leon."

"But--"

"Now," Jason said crisply.

Leon rather reluctantly reached behind him and produced the rifle, which he handed to Wolfe.

"Thank you."

"What we would like," Jason said, "is for you to come with us and meet our leader."

"Leader? Of what?"

Jason smiled. "Nothing sinister, I assure you, Mr. Wolfe. It's just—you could call it a protective society. Don't worry. He'll explain everything when we get there." Jason stood and Leon quickly followed suit. "Can we help you get your gear together? Then we'll show you where we live. You'll like it. You might even want to join us."

Wolfe said nothing, but he knew better than that. Whatever this society of theirs was, and wherever they lived, they could not compare with his own family waiting for him several thousand miles away on the Gulf Coast of Florida. It took him only a few moments to roll his things together and stuff everything into the rucksack. "All right," he said when he was ready. Then he grinned and added, "Take me to your leader."

Neither of the young men so much as cracked a smile, although Wolfe had thought it a pretty good line. The two set off at a swift walk with Wolfe and the dog trailing behind.

CHAPTER FOUR

Two sharp turns and about three miles down the floor of the canyon Wolfe had been following, they came to a footpath leading up to a bridge that spanned the width of the canyon. At the top of the bridge lay a small town, unlike any town Wolfe had seen since he emerged from hiding after the nuclear war. This one was still functioning.

There were no trucks or automobiles in evidence. He was used to not seeing any vehicles in motion, but here, he did not even see any abandoned along the streets. What he did see were horses. Mostly, they were hitched to low-riding, sturdy wagons, but a few saddle horses were tied to rails in front of the buildings, just like something out of an old western movie.

"Oh, we cleared all that away," Jason told him when Wolfe asked about the missing vehicles. "They just got in the way. We pulled them over to that end of town and stuck them in a vacant lot there. You never know what pieces you might want off of 'em. The older ones, the ones with frames instead of unibody construction, were mostly converted into those wagons you see there."

"Clever," Wolfe said, and he meant it.

"Our leader is very clever. You see all the windmills?"

"It would have been difficult to miss them." Most buildings in the town had what looked like the windmills used to pump water in isolated pastures and the more empty stretches in the west. Except instead of standing on towers, perched over wells, these were, for the most part, mounted on roofs.

"That was our leader's idea, too," Jason said. "While we still had gasoline available, we gathered those in from ranches for a hundred miles around. We took them apart and brought them here. Now they're turning generators that we removed from those cars and trucks I mentioned before. The generators feed banks of batteries in each house or store, and we converted our power to twelve volt, so now we have electric lights and workable small appliances, even a little refrigeration."

"Air conditioning?" Wolfe asked, rather hopefully. It was late afternoon and the heat was stifling.

Jason laughed. "We don't have that much power available, but we do have electric fans. They help a lot."

"Tell me more about this leader of yours."

"He'll tell you whatever he wants you to know. Down this way, please." Jason led the way to a stone courthouse building set in a small square in the center of town.

There was a bronze statue in the yard, depicting a doughboy from World War I, and several smaller marble plinths, carrying messages of dedication to those who served in World War II, Korea, Vietnam, and the Gulf Wars. Wolfe wondered if anyone would get around to adding one in honor of the servicemen and women who were in uniform for this latest war, also.

It occurred to him that he did not even know what this last war was being called. He wished he did.

"This way," Jason said when they got inside.

The interior of the stone building was noticeably cooler. The walls were painted institutional green and their footsteps echoed hollowly on the hardwood floors.

Leon stopped at the entrance and took up a position there as if he were guarding it. To keep the newcomer from escaping? The question leaped rather uncharitably into Wolfe's thoughts.

They passed a water cooler and Wolfe stopped beside it. "I don't suppose this thing is working?" he asked, hopefully.

"Afraid not," Jason said. "We haven't figured out how to make those work on twelve volts and they don't seem worth using one of the few plug-in converters that we have. Or is that inverters? I can never remember. Not that it matters."

"No."

"In here, please."

There was a light spot on the door to show where a sign once had been, but the sign had been removed and not replaced with anything else. The sign almost certainly would have pointed out a courtroom—district court or circuit or whatever it used to be here. The layout inside the large, very high-ceilinged room was that of a typical courtroom, with the judge's bench at the head of the room, jury box and witness boxes, and a polished wood bar separating that working part of the room from the spectator's benches that occupied most of the floor.

The customary tables for opposing counsel had been removed along with the chairs that would have been there. The usual American and state flags were also missing. But, a pair of electric fans whirred and turned on either side of the judge's high, handsome bench.

At the bench, seated there as if on a throne, sat the leader Jason so lovingly referred to. Wolfe wondered if he was expected to genuflect or kowtow or some such foolishness.

But he did stop just inside the door and stared for a moment. He couldn't help himself. The sight of the leader was…well, not what he expected.

CHAPTER FIVE

"You can put your things down over there, please." Jason laid his own weapon on one of the spectator benches, and Wolfe quickly stripped off his rucksack and put it down with a clatter, then leaned his rifle against it.

He motioned for the dog to sit beside his things and guard them. The dog sat; it remained to be seen for how long he would stay that way. He was not exactly known for his diligence when it came to Wolfe's personal security, after all.

Wolfe stood as straight as he could and unconsciously reached up with both hands to smooth his hair back. If he'd known what to expect here, he would have tied it back in a ponytail or... or something. For the first time in a very long while, he was concerned about his appearance. For the first time since the beginning of the war, he supposed. But, now...

"Mistress Alethia?" Jason said, "May I present this stranger who has come among us?" The young man bowed.

Wolfe was not sure how he was supposed to respond, or if he should do anything at all. He stood there feeling as awkward as a schoolboy with his hands pressed tight to his sides and his palms sweating. He tried, with very limited success, to swallow back a lump that had sprung up in his throat.

Jason remained bent over in the bow and backed away a couple steps before straightening again. Wolfe was left standing there alone. He was staring.

Mistress Alethia was—well, she was scarcely believable. No human being could be that radiantly beautiful. The woman could have been aged between twenty to forty—or beyond. She had a huge mane of softly curling hair the color of a fiery sunset. It surrounded a face that had truly patrician features: long slender column of pale neck; high cheekbones; exceptionally full lips; huge green eyes set amid delicate curly eyelashes; slim, straight nose. She looked like something one would see on a magazine cover or projected twenty times life-size onto a movie screen. Wolfe had never in his life seen any woman so beautiful as this. Just looking at her made it difficult for him to breathe.

Jason, who certainly was already familiar with her, looked like he wanted to drop to his knees and worship her. Of course, for all Wolfe knew, maybe this band of survivors did worship their Mistress Alethia. Certainly, they viewed her as something very special, someone far beyond the ordinary, far above the ordinary.

"Welcome," she said in a husky voice that was just short of being a purr, but the purr of a lioness, not a housecat. "Do not give me the name you once carried. I do not want to know. You have the look of a wild thing from the dark forests. You look like a wolf, and that is what I shall call you. From now on, for as long as you remain among us, your name is Wolf."

Wolfe wondered if someone, Leon, perhaps, had hurried ahead to tell her what his name was so that she could give herself an aura of mysticism. The truth, however, was that he doubted very much that any such thing happened, and he felt a shiver run along his spine.

Jason glanced up sharply and his mouth dropped open as if he wanted to speak—as if he wanted to tell this Mistress Alethia that the stranger's name indeed was Wolfe. But the young man said nothing.

"What skills do you bring to us, Wolf?" the glorious leader asked.

"I have no particular skills," Wolfe told her, feeling more comfortable with the situation now. After all, she was a woman. She was only mortal. "I'm passing through, that's all."

"You accept the name 'Wolf'?"

"It is my name," he said calmly. Although, his meaning when he said it and the meaning she was apt to put on the words were two entirely different things. His comment was literal. He was aware that Mistress Alethia would very likely take his words as an acceptance of her right to name him—and to claim him? No, not that. He was no man's property. And no woman's. He only wanted to pass by on his way back home.

"Welcome, Wolf. Welcome to Paradise."

He smiled just a little. This was one thing Mistress Alethia was surely wrong about. Paradise was not here in the barrens of Utah. True paradise was far away from this place. Paradise was wherever Lurleen and Jojo were at this moment. With that thought, Mistress Alethia's beauty lost its grip on him, and he was able to regard her as just another human being. Prettier than most, perhaps, but with no power to enthrall.

"Thanks." The word was perfunctory, his voice indifferent. "Thanks."

CHAPTER SIX

"I'll take you to your quarters now," Jason said.

"Thanks, but I don't intend to stay. I appreciate you bringing me this far, and I'd like to fill my canteens from one of your wells, but that's all I need. I'll be on my way."

"The leader wishes you'd stay."

"That leader won't remember who I am by tomorrow evening. I'm sure she won't miss me at all."

Jason said nothing. He picked up his rifle from the bench seat close to the door. The dog wagged its tail and looked like it was smiling. Wolfe reached past the dog to take hold of his rucksack and rifle. They were gone, the bench empty where he had placed them minutes earlier.

He gave Jason a sharp look. Jason acted as if he had no idea what had caused Wolfe's displeasure. Wolfe spun around to snap at Mistress Alethia, but the beautiful redhead was gone, the throne-like judge's bench at the front of the room, empty, with not so much as a scrap of paper to be seen on it.

"Hey! Dammit!" Wolfe barked.

"Follow me, please. Will you go to your quarters?"

"Are my things there? What happened to my rucksack and rifle and bow?"

"I don't know where those things are right now. You could see for yourself, I didn't take them."

"Fine. Who did?"

"We have more than a hundred souls here. I'm sure they acted properly, every one of them. Now, please, come with me."

He could do no more than follow Jason and allow the young man to cage him in some sort of transient quarters, or whatever they were. Wolfe fully intended to reclaim his belongings—God knew there were few enough of them and of little value—and leave Mistress Alethia's so-called 'Paradise' behind.

CHAPTER SEVEN

Jason led the way outdoors. There was no sign of Leon, although a number of other people, all of them quite young, were in view on the streets of Paradise. They all looked fit to the point of being downright athletic, and all carried rifles. A few also wore pistols on their belts.

"Can I ask you something?" Jason said as they went down the courthouse steps to the sidewalk.

"I don't have anything to hide."

"How come you keep putting those heavy goggles on and taking them off again?"

"My eyes are kind of sensitive to sunlight, that's all," Wolfe said, fully aware that he was indeed hiding something with that statement, but then he saw no reason why he should tell these people about his ability to see in the dark.

Jason accepted the explanation without apparent interest, and led the way to a tall, narrow building with a freshly-painted signboard reading, 'Paradise Hotel'. It was set on a downtown street corner.

On the side street, there was a no-parking zone, and beside it, a metal sign saying, 'Bus Stop.'

"New resident," Jason announced as they entered.

A slender young man with prematurely thinning hair got up from an armchair where he'd been reading, and came over to rummage in a drawer behind the check-in counter. "Number thirty-two," he said, handing over a key.

Wolfe could not see why keys would be necessary here. There would be duplicates at the desk for anyone who wanted into his room. Besides, it seemed that around here, people stole in broad daylight anyway. Otherwise, his rifle and bow and rucksack would not be missing.

"Your room is at the top of the stairs," the desk clerk said. "Just don't use the toilet. The water doesn't work above the first floor. When you need the bathroom, there's one in that room over there." He pointed. "If it helps any, we hooked up one of those instant shower heater things out of a motor home. You can use all the hot water you want."

"That sounds good."

"You'll be wanting clean clothes. I'll bring some up to you later." The fellow scrutinized him with a critical eye. "Extra large shirt, I'd say. Though, you don't look it from a distance. Waist, about…what? Thirty-two?"

"Thirty," Wolfe said.

"Shoe size?"

"Shoes too?"

"Why not? Those look pretty ragged."

Wolfe hadn't been paying all that much attention, but the miles and miles of walking he'd been doing since returning to the outside world had done nothing for his sneakers, but he'd traded those for FEDCOM boots less than a week prior. They were still in good shape and freshly broken in. "No need. It's just dust on these, but I wear a ten and a half, just in case I have a blow out," he replied.

"Are you hungry?" Jason asked.

"As a bear," Wolfe told him.

"Think you can scare up a sandwich for him, Buddy?"

The clerk nodded. "Sure."

"Sandwich?" Wolfe asked. "You have bread?"

"Don't expect it to be soft, white Wonderbread, but, yes, we have bread. We have a good supply of flour, and bake our own in wood-burning ovens. Sweet rolls, too. Pies. Cakes. The apples'll be coming ripe soon, and I'm looking forward to some fresh apple pie." Buddy grinned. "In the meantime, we have to make do with dried apple pie."

"You have it better here than people do back in the clear area. How do you manage that?"

Buddy only grinned again and led Wolfe to the hotel dining room, where he found an insulated carafe of actual, honest to Pete, for real coffee. Brewed coffee, too. Not that instant junk.

"Help yourself," Buddy said. "Can't offer you fresh milk, but we have powdered creamer and all the sugar you'd care for."

"Good Lord!" Wolfe blurted.

"Oh, we manage to scrape along," Buddy said.

Wolfe intended to ask Jason again about his rucksack and things, but when he turned to speak to the young man, Jason was nowhere in sight. People did seem to come and go around here according to a plan that Wolfe wasn't part of. For the moment, that did not seem all that important. Real coffee? With creamer? And real sugar? It wouldn't hurt a thing, he decided, to layover here for a few days while he rested and tried to put the ugliness with the Alstons and Thelma White behind him. No, sir! That would not hurt a darned thing.

"You said something about sandwiches?" he reminded Buddy. "And coffee."

"Right over here," Buddy said, taking him across the room to a long table, where plates and platters and bowls of pre-war delights bulged. At that particular moment, Wolfe was not sure this was, in fact, not paradise.

CHAPTER EIGHT

With his belly full to the point of groaning, Wolfe made his way up a set of old creaking wooden stairs to the third floor, the dog at his side. The dog seemed to have enjoyed the lunch downstairs as much as Wolfe did. He took another step and winced at how much noise the dried-out treads made. No one was going to sneak up or down this staircase without announcing his presence. He wondered how old the building was. It could be more than a hundred years, he guessed. Well, maybe.

Room thirty-two was to the right of the third-floor landing. There was one more floor above his—four floors. Could they build buildings that tall a hundred years ago? He didn't know. Not that it mattered.

The room was about as old-fashioned as everything else in the hotel. It had a narrow bed with an iron headboard. The bed had sheets on it and a rather thin wool blanket. The pillow was grey with age and nearly flat. There was a plain oak wardrobe, a straight-backed chair, and a small stand that held a basin and pitcher. Beneath the bed was an actual thunder mug. Wolfe had seen those before, but only in museums and movies.

This place, he thought, would not be out of place in a western film. John Wayne, Clint Eastwood—what was the name of that other guy he used to see so much? George Kennedy. That was it. The room looked like a movie set for one of those guys.

"I'll take the bed," he said to the dog, which wagged its tail at the sound of his voice. "You can have the rug, okay?"

He lifted the lid on the thunder mug. It was clean and shiny, but did not look substantial enough for its purpose. There was water in the pitcher. He dipped a finger into it. It was tepid, of course—room temperature. Wolfe idly wondered if these people had figured out how to make ice these days. What wouldn't he give for a big paper cup of Pepsi just loaded with tiny ice cubes?

"Well, well, well," he muttered aloud when he opened the doors of the wardrobe, and heard the dog's tail thump on the floor in response. His rucksack was propped inside the wardrobe with the bow and aluminum blowgun still lashed to its sides. There was no sign of the rifle. Apparently, whoever did the stealing around here did not think a blowgun or a bow were dangerous enough to be worth bothering with.

Out of curiosity, he pulled the ruck out, and opened it so he could root around inside. The magazines of 223 ammunition for his M16 were missing. Even so, he was glad to have most of his things back, and the supply of foods he had taken from Thelma White's place was there. If worst came to worst, he could always abandon the rifle and take off again with just what he had right now. He had been in far worse shape than this when he first set out, and he'd made it this far. He could get along again without a firearm if he had to.

It would soon be completely dark outside, and the only

light he could see in the room was an overhead electric fixture left over from the days when there was real electricity and a real world for it to power, not this crazy movie set place.

Wolfe changed his opinion, though. The Paradise Hotel was not something out of a western, he decided. Instead, it was suitable for one of those futuristic horror shows. He kicked his shoes off and pulled the dark goggles down so they hung at his throat. This was his time of day now. But he did not necessarily want Mistress Alethia's subjects, or whatever the heck they were, to know that. He lay back on the bed—the springs creaked almost as badly as the stair steps had—and cleared his throat.

"All right. You can get up here, too. But, no snoring, you hear?"

He patted the mattress by his side, and the dog jumped up without waiting for a second invitation.

CHAPTER NINE

Whe Wolfe got up in the morning and started downstairs to the bathroom, he found a stack of clothing outside his door. Apparently, Buddy, or perhaps one of the others who lived and worked here, delivered them during the night but hadn't wanted to intrude while Wolfe was sleeping. He had half a dozen undershorts—jockey-style, not boxers—two pairs of brand-new Levis, four athletic grey sweatshirts, and six pairs of socks. Of greatest interest to him was a pair of new walking shoes with heavily-cushioned soles, and Velcro instead of laces. There were also two white towels and a pair of washcloths. Plus, a personal grooming set of the kind that hotels and airlines used to hand out with the tiny tubes of toothpaste, half-sized toothbrush, paper-wrapped wafer of Ivory soap and a disposable razor. Not that Wolfe needed to shave. His beard no longer grew, although he did not know why.

"Looks like we're all set," he said to the dog. "Except for some flea shampoo. You'd think they would have thought of that, wouldn't you?"

He carried everything back into his room, and selected

the things he would need downstairs for a shower and change of clothing. Twenty minutes later when he stepped out of the bathroom, he felt a new man. Or, more accurately, he felt like the old one, the one who existed before the war. Hot water! Imagine that!

"You would be Wolf," another of the fit and healthy-looking young men said to him. "I'm Tavis. I'll show you around today. Tomorrow you can begin work."

"Work?"

Tavis smiled. "The leader has not told me what she plans for you, Wolf, but I know it will be something useful. Something you're capable of doing for the good of us all here in Paradise."

"What do you do when you aren't guiding strangers around the place?"

"I'm an irrigation technician," Tavis said.

"Irrigating what?"

"You'll see. You will see everything. But first, let's have some breakfast, shall we?"

Breakfast consisted of Wheaties. The crunchy flakes were beginning to turn limp and stale with age, despite having been sealed in their boxes since sometime before the war. Even so, they tasted good soaked in canned milk and covered with sugar. Tavis offered no objection when Wolfe prepared a bowl for the dog, too, complete with milk and sugar.

"You have it good here," Wolfe observed over his third cup of real coffee.

"As a matter of fact, we do."

"How do you manage?"

Tavis smiled. "There is no secret about it. There were lots of warehouses in the Salt Lake City area. People scavenge goods out of those and bring them to us for trade."

"You mentioned irrigation earlier. Are you growing crops

here somewhere and trading fresh goods for manufactured ones?"

"Something along those lines," Tavis told him. "And, we do grow a few things, although mostly for our own use. What we are raising here, what people desperately want now, is horses—cattle, too, to some extent. But our real wealth is in our horses."

"The land around here is desert," Wolfe blurted. "How could you raise horses on it?"

"We raise alfalfa on the flats beside the river," Tavis said. "That is what we're irrigating. And we feed the horses and cattle with that alfalfa."

"It didn't take this Mistress Alethia of yours long to establish such a complex arrangement. The war was only two years ago."

"That's right. But the leader is far-seeing. Immediately after the war, she looked around and saw the potential here. She put her plan into effect at once. You see the result around you. Or, anyway, you will, as soon as we finish here."

"I'm done," Wolfe said, pushing his empty bowl away. He felt good, actually. Clean and refreshed. In a way, it was a shame he would have to leave. But he did have to leave. He had to find Lurleen and Jojo. Or, at least determine that he never would. "Lead on, friend Tavis."

The dog jumped up and walked close by Wolfe's side as they headed out to meet the new day.

CHAPTER TEN

"Tell me something, Wolf," Tavis asked several hours later. "...if you don't mind."

They were taking a break from walking several miles in the heat so they could look over the town and the fields surrounding it. At the moment, they were sitting atop a high bluff overlooking the small, very green valley, with the thin silver ribbon of water running through it.

"Ask away," Wolfe offered.

"What do you think of the regulators?"

The oddity of the question took Wolfe by surprise and he had to think for a moment to work out what Tavis meant. "The clocks, you mean? What do I think of regulator clocks?"

"That is what the term 'regulator' means to you, Wolf?" Tavis asked.

"Sure. I suppose it could be applied to some other things, too, of course. Mechanical, electrical—I'm sure lots of things would have parts that would be regulators. Toasters—now there's something I haven't had reason to think of for a long time." He scratched the dog under the chin and the animal leaned against his legs. "Isn't a regulator what you call the part that tells the toast when to pop up?"

Tavis laughed. "I'll take your word for it."

"How do you mean it?" Wolfe asked him.

Tavis shrugged and laughed again. "It was a nonsense question. I didn't mean anything by it."

"If you say so." Wolfe did not believe that, not for a minute. The question had been serious. He was certain of that. But he did not know what his answer was supposed to be.

"Anyway, you can see down there our real goal: alfalfa. The horses are over there." Tavis pointed north. "They're inside the canyon with all the clean water they could ever want, and, close by, the alfalfa. We can protect them from predators."

"Or thieves?" Wolfe asked.

"Of course. But, then, those are just another predator, aren't they?"

"I suppose so. What will you be doing, then? Selling the horses?"

"Of course. We started a breeding program. A few of our mares were already in foal when we acquired them last fall, so we already have some babies on the ground. And, we've been breeding all our mares this season. Next year, we expect to have a good crop. In the meantime, we have a few geldings that we can sell or lease."

"Lease?" Wolfe asked.

"Why not? Civilization didn't stop because of the war, you know? It only changed. And commerce goes on, regardless."

"I guess it does, at that," Wolfe conceded. "What will happen when those warehouses have been emptied and there are no more pre-war goods to be had?"

"The leader will have an answer to meet our needs. She already has something in mind, I'm sure."

"I see. There's something that just struck me. So far, I've only seen young men in Paradise. What happened to the old and the very young? What happened to all the women?"

"The town had been abandoned when the leader decided to occupy it and surround herself with her chosen few. Not all are men, though. There are women—a few. They cook and clean and they provide, uh…other necessary services, also. Each man in Paradise is allowed to visit them when he feels the urge. You're new and haven't yet earned your keep, but perhaps you would be allowed to visit with a woman." Tavis smiled. "When we get back, I'll ask, and if it's all right, I'll take you over there."

"You're very kind," Wolfe said. He was beginning to have some very serious reservations about Paradise and its people, and was glad he would not be staying. This afternoon, he thought, he would try to get a little sleep and tonight when he could see comfortably, he would take his things and go, with or without the missing rifle.

CHAPTER ELEVEN

Wolfe lay on the bed, the dog snoring, actually snoring at his side, when someone tapped lightly on the door.

"Come in."

Tavis opened the door a crack and peeped in shyly. "Did I wake you?"

"No, I was just thinking."

The dog woke up and yawned. Tavis gave its teeth a rather apprehensive look. They did look wicked, Wolfe thought. Worked mighty well, too. They certainly had slashed Ed Alston's cheek wide open despite the animal's normally placid demeanor. Maybe Tavis was wise to be wary of someone else's dog.

"We can complete that tour now if you feel like it," the young man said.

Wolfe thought that they'd done that this morning. Not that there was so very much to see—fields, barns, and horses outside the town, and a collection of sun-baked wooden buildings inside it. None of it seemed all that interesting to

Wolfe, but then, he had no real interest in the place. He was only passing through on his way home to his family.

He sat up and slid his feet into his new shoes. Lordy, but they were comfortable!

The dog jumped off the bed and wagged its tail. It was ready to go whether he was or not.

"Can you leave him here?" Tavis asked, pointing to the dog. "I don't think…well, I just don't think it would be a good idea."

Wolfe shrugged and motioned for the dog to stay. It sighed but settled obediently onto the rug. Wolfe suspected it would be back onto the bed before he and Tavis reached the stairs, but he didn't really mind. Truth was that he was becoming fond of the animal.

"After you," he said, and pulled the door closed behind him as he followed Tavis into the third-floor hallway.

CHAPTER TWELVE

Tavis flagged down a passing wagon and the driver pulled his team of thin, rather shaggy-looking horses to a stop so that they could hop onto the tailgate. They sat with their legs dangling off the back of the ancient and sun-bleached farm wagon. Wolfe was reminded of the time when he was a boy and they went on a hayride in the fall. He could not remember the occasion, but guessed it had something to do with Halloween, or possibly Thanksgiving.

The driver shook his reins and the pair of horses started forward, the wagon lurching so hard that Wolfe almost lost his balance and fell off.

"Are you all right?"

"Fine, thanks."

"I should have warned you."

It felt strange to be riding after all this time. Even the walking pace of a horse-drawn wagon felt oddly swift.

If he had a horse, Wolfe realized, he could make it home much faster than by walking. On the other hand, he knew nothing about horses except what he'd seen on television. He suspected that having watched a few cowboy shows on the tube was not enough to earn him any credits in the school of horse husbandry. Still, it would be nice.

"We only use the geldings to pull vehicles or work under saddle," Tavis was explaining. "All the breeding stock is kept in the valley back there where I showed you. They're under armed guard day and night."

"You have to guard them?" Wolfe asked.

"Predators," Tavis said, then turned his head away to look at the buildings they were passing. After a half-mile or so, the wagon turned the corner and Tavis called out, "We'll get off here, Barry."

The driver signaled the horses to stop and the two tail-gate passengers slid down to the ground.

"Thanks, Barry."

"Thank you, Mister."

The wagon rattled off about its business and Tavis led Wolfe to what used to be a motel, although the line of low, concrete block cabins seemed old enough to have been a motor court when it was new, back before the term 'motel' was even coined.

"What's this?" Wolfe asked.

Tavis snickered. "You'll see." He entered the office and tapped a bell on the counter.

CHAPTER THIRTEEN

The man who emerged from a room at the back of the office looked like a weightlifter, Wolfe thought, or perhaps one of those California surfer boys who spent all their time on the beach working out with weights. He was blond, with bulging muscles and a deep tan. He was carrying a spiral-bound notebook and a pen.

"This is the man called Wolf. He's a guest. The leader said he should be given a visit here to get acquainted."

"Oh, yes," the beach boy said.

Wolfe was entering his forties and trying not to show it.

"I heard he would be coming. What about you, Tavis? You want your turn now?"

"Sure. Why not?"

The man behind the counter opened his book and began searching through it.

Tavis turned to Wolfe. "Each of us is entitled to one visit per week," he explained. "Andrew here keeps track to make sure no one is abusing the privileges. Of course, we can earn extra visits if the leader thinks we deserve them. Or our visits could be taken away for disciplinary reasons."

"I see," Wolfe said, not at all sure that he did understand. So far, all he saw was a run-down old motel.

Andrew found whatever he was looking for in the notebook and made a mark, presumably checking off Tavis for his week's visit to the motel. He closed the book and laid it on the counter, pulled open a drawer and brought out two room keys. He handed one to Tavis, checked the number on the tag, and gave the other to Wolfe. "Have fun."

"Thank you." Still puzzled, Wolfe followed Tavis back outside.

"Just go to the room number on your key and go inside. It's yours until morning." Tavis, smiling and obviously eager now, hurried down the row of motor court cabins to find his.

Wolfe glanced at the key in his hand. The oblong, plastic tag had a large number '3' on it. "Cabin three, then. Fine." Wolfe suspected he knew now what he would find there. He hoped he was wrong. The door stuck slightly when he tried to open it. He gave it a shove and entered.

The cabin smelled musty with age, but there was nothing old about the girl who sat on the side of the bed inside. She was in her late teens or early twenties, Wolfe guessed, with long, red hair, a pretty face, and a very generously endowed figure. Wolfe could see that figure quite well, as she was naked.

She sat facing away from him. He was not sure, but he thought she was trembling. He stepped in and closed the door behind him.

CHAPTER FOURTEEN

Wolfe walked around to the far side of the bed where she was seated. When he reached her, she sat still without looking at him. She made no attempt to cover herself.

"Would you stand up for a moment, please?"

She did so, moving mechanically, head and eyes down. Wolfe reached behind her and pulled the sheet off the bed. He spread it out wide and wrapped it around her. The girl's eyes found him then, wide with inquiry. Wolfe smiled at her.

"You're a lovely girl, but I'm a married man." The smile turned into a grin. "We wouldn't want to push this tempta-tion thing too far, would we?" He gestured. "Sit down, why don't you? Relax. My name is Wolfe and I'd like to talk with you tonight."

The girl nodded and sat rather gingerly on the edge of the bed as if poised to flee if need be. "I can see why she calls you Wolf. There is something about you. I mean, you look like a very nice man, but…I hope you don't get mad at me, Wolf."

He laughed. "My name has nothing to do with that pretentious woman who calls herself—what was it, again?

Alethia? No, my name really is Wolfe—with an 'e'. Jim Wolfe. And I'm just passing through, trying to get home to my family."

"Then you aren't—" She did not finish the sentence.

"I'm not what?" he asked.

"They told me I'd be entertaining you. I'm supposed to question you. You know, bed talk. The leader doesn't trust you. She wants to know more about you."

"All she had to do was ask."

"Oh, she wouldn't trust anything you just up and told her."

"Funny, I've often found that people who are not trusting of others are often not trustworthy themselves."

The girl glanced around as if afraid they were being overheard.

"Is the room wired?"

She shook her head. "No. They would, but there isn't enough power right now, and they can't find all the snooper gadgets they want. They know where some are, but there's too much radiation. It wouldn't be safe to use them."

"Would you mind telling me more about the place, then?"

"You aren't—" She looked frightened, and he thought she shuddered, her shoulders shaking just a little beneath the loosely wrapped sheet.

Wolfe raised an eyebrow and waited for her to continue.

"You aren't here to try and trick me into something, are you?"

"Of course not. Why would I do that?"

"I told you. She doesn't trust people. Last week there was a man. He was asking a lot of questions. I think maybe he was trying to see if I'm loyal."

"And, are you? Loyal, I mean?"

She made a face. "God, no. I'd be away from here in a heartbeat if I could."

"What's stopping you?"

"You don't know? You really don't?"

"No. That's why I asked."

"Mr. Wolfe, Mistress Alethia's 'Paradise' is a trap. It is a horrid place where everyone exists just to do her bidding. She's an evil person, Mr. Wolfe, truly evil, and that is not a word I use lightly. She's evil just like it says in the Bible—that kind of evil."

"I'd like you to tell me about Paradise, please." He smiled. "But, first, if you don't mind, I'd like you to tell me your name. Then, maybe we can help each other, because I don't know nearly enough about Paradise. But I do know that I'll be leaving here—tonight, if possible—tomorrow night, at the very latest. If you want to leave with me, you're welcome to come along."

CHAPTER FIFTEEN

"My name is Rebecca Morrison. Everybody calls me Becca, or they did." Her nose wrinkled with disgust. "She named me 'Blossom', so that's what everybody here calls me now, and I hate it. And she had me put this gunk on my hair to make it red like hers. Hmph! Hers is as fake as this color. My hair is really brown. Kind of mouse brown, but I don't mind that. It's my real color, and I was happy with it. The leader, she has something about red hair, so she made me color mine. And made me do this—reward the workers. That's what they call it. It isn't prostitution. It's a nice way to reward the faithful. I want to puke every time somebody walks through that door."

"You can't say no?" Wolfe asked.

"Oh, I tried. In the beginning, I tried. Alethia, or whatever her name really is, she knows… she knows how to hurt people. Hurt them really, really bad, in ways, in places, that you don't want to know."

"She hurt you?"

Becca nodded. "Three times. The last time was—I

couldn't bear to go through that again, Mr. Wolfe. Is it all right if I call you Jim?"

"Of course."

"I couldn't stand for her to do that to me again, Jim, so I've been…I've done whatever she wants of me ever since then. She says I'm pretty. I don't think so, but she uses me when she wants to get information out of somebody, or wants to give them something special. She taught me things that—I hate it, Jim. I hate it so bad sometimes I wish I had some way to kill myself. If I can't get away any other way, I guess someday I'll do that."

"I hope it won't come to that. But what is with her? How did she get power over all these people?"

"I don't know that I can really explain that. She came here just after the war. She showed up driving a camper with New York license plates. By then, there were only a few people left living here. Most took off after the Salt Lake City bombs went off. There were four of them, bombs, I mean, and we're close enough that most everyone thought the fallout would kill us if we stayed. I would have gone too, but—"

"You are from here, then?"

"Oh, yes. One of the few. The town isn't really called Paradise. That's just what she named it. It's really Tifton."

"Tifton…what?"

"That's all. Just Tifton."

He smiled. "No, I meant, like, in what state?"

"You don't know what state you're in?"

"Not that it really matters, but no, I don't." It was the first time he saw her smile.

She laughed a little and said, "We're in Wyoming. Just barely, but this is Wyoming. If you go down that way," she pointed, "you're in Utah. Over there a little and you're in Colorado. But, right here, we're in good old Wyoming."

"Tifton. I don't remember seeing it on the map."

"That's the story of my life. Too unimportant to make me noticed, including now."

"You were telling me about this leader thing, and how Paradise got started."

"Yeah, right. Well, we were little old Tifton, Wyoming, then, and there was the war and nearly everybody took off. Some said they were going to Canada, some to Cheyenne, which I thought was kind of silly, because surely there were missiles targeted at the Air Force Base outside Cheyenne. But, anyway, people wanted to get out of here. They filled up with gasoline while they could and left."

"Why did you stay?"

"I would have gone with them except for my father. He was dying and somebody had to stay with him, so I did." She shrugged.

"I see."

"Then, the next thing I knew, she was here. And there were some people who came through. People who were running away from Salt Lake and what was left around there. I guess it's pretty bad on the other side of the mountains over there. There isn't much left. So everybody there ran in this direction. And some of them, mostly young men, Alethia roped in and put under her spell. Now she controls them. She controls all of us in Paradise. She wants to control everything and everybody for miles around, and she does, except for the Regulators."

"Regulators?" he repeated. "That's the second time I've heard that term. What does it mean?"

"The Regulators are what they call themselves. They're a bunch of people—old folks, a lot of them, like you—who refuse to be dominated by Alethia. They live...I don't know where they live! If I did, I think I'd go there and see if they'd take me in. Mostly, they're folks who used to live around here. They resent her, you see, when she was setting things up, Alethia confiscated all the gasoline that was still available. She had her tame worker ants dig up the storage tanks at the gas stations, and go around to the farms and ranches in the area, emptying all the gasoline storage tanks they kept for their machinery. She grabbed up all the gasoline, the horses, whatever other livestock she wanted, and for sure all the windmills. That's the thing, you see. With no electric power and no way to refill the propane tanks like on some of the pumps, she controls the water because of the windmills. She uses some of the windmills to pump water for here, and the rest of them to power generators she took off cars and trucks. Lord knows there's enough abandoned cars and trucks to cannibalize. So, while there was still gas she could use for making raids far off from Tifton, she stole every windmill and every horse and everything she wanted. The Regulators, I think, are mostly folks that she stole this stuff from, and she was afraid that you might be a spy for the Regulators, Jim, you being an old guy—no offense intended."

He smiled a little but did not bother to correct her. He tended to forget that his hair was snowy white, but it obviously made everyone else think of him as an old man. "No offense taken," he assured her.

"These Regulators," he asked, "Is that why everyone around here carries guns?"

"Mostly, yes. It used to be that there would be scavengers and wilders coming through, and they might be a danger. Not now, though. The scavengers she recruited so they'd bring her the things they take from the red zones and trade with her. She set up almost a clearing house sort of thing for stuff moving in and out of the clear area. As for the wilders, they're her kind of people. She took a lot of them in and made them part of her little Paradise empire. The ones that wouldn't knuckle under to her, she had disposed of."

"Disposed of?"

"Shot," Becca explained. "She had them executed out at the town dump. There must be, I don't know, a couple dozen bodies out there. She just tossed them on a trash heap and let the birds and coyotes have them."

"Nice lady," Wolfe said.

"A real princess," Becca agreed.

"You could end up on that trash heap, too, if you decide to go with me," Wolfe cautioned.

She nodded. "I know. But, do you know what? I'd rather do that than spend the rest of my days here, like this. You've given me hope, Jim. I haven't had any of that for a very long time."

"What about your father? Will he be coming along too?"

She sighed. "My dad died six months ago. He loved this place. To him, Tifton really was a sort of paradise, I think. It was so quiet, and everyone was decent and cared about each other. We weren't family, and we had our quarrels and little feuds and things, but it was a good town, and there were good people here. I suppose it's something of a blessing that he didn't live to see what Alethia turned it into."

Wolfe patted her hand and gave her a moment of silence with her memories, then said, "If you're sure you want to come with me, Becca, I think we need to put our heads together and make some plans for getting out of here."

"I'm sure," she said. "No matter what happens, I want to come."

"All right, then. I want you to tell me everything you know about the way Paradise is guarded from these Regulators. And is there something to drink in here?"

"There's stuff in the closet. Whiskey, some wine. There isn't any beer left, though."

"I was hoping for something a little softer. Water would be all right."

"Would a soft drink do? I have some of those. Most of the men who come here want liquor, not sodas."

"Child, I would kill for a Pepsi at this moment! Well… sort of."

"I'm out of regular Coke and Pepsi, but I think there's some diet sodas. Pepsi One, Mountain Dew, and—"

"Oh, my! It could be this is paradise after all." He laughed and eagerly accepted a plastic bottle of Pepsi One that Becca fetched from the room's tiny closet. There were beverages and snacks in there, he noticed, but no clothing. Apparently, Becca was not permitted any clothes in her workplace. That, he decided, was about to change.

The only thing remaining was to determine when and how to leave. Although, considering that business about the town dump, and the fate of those passersby who did not see things Alethia's way, leaving might not be as easy as he'd expected. He opened the soft drink and took a swallow. It had to be the best thing he'd tasted since before the war. "Do me a favor."

"Sure. What?"

"Pull that sheet a little tighter around you, would you please? It's starting to gape open there and make me uncomfortable."

Becca blushed and hurriedly wrapped the sheet close around her.

CHAPTER SIXTEEN

"Good morning, Wolfe!" the man in the hotel lobby said. "Did you have a nice time?"

Wolfe smiled. "Very nice! Thank you, Buddy." And it was the truth, even though neither Buddy nor any of his friends would likely guess what sort of a nice time he'd had with Becca during the long night hours. "Very nice, indeed."

Wolfe went up to his room and immediately brought the dog down so it could go outside and get some relief after being locked up overnight. Then, he and the dog went into breakfast and some more of that real coffee. If there was one thing about Paradise that he would miss, it would be the coffee.

When he emerged from the dining room after breakfast, Buddy was no longer in the lobby, but there was a man lounging in one of the chairs, reading a tattered Reader's Digest from before the war. The fellow looked up, and, without rising, said, "You're Wolf, right?"

Wolfe nodded.

"You're 'sposed to wait here. The leader will want to see you after a while."

"Can I wait upstairs?" He smiled. "I'd like to get a little rest after…after last night."

"Sure. Someone will call you when the leader is ready."

Wolfe tapped his thigh to get the dog's attention and returned to his third-floor room. He pulled the blinds to make the room dark so he could remove the goggles, and set about making preparations to leave. The rucksack was already packed and ready to go. The bow and blowgun were still strapped to it. He would have liked to have kept the rifle, but that seemed to have been confiscated, and he did not want to arouse any suspicions by demanding its return.

He did go through the things in the ruck to make sure everything was there, then tightened the straps and bindings to make the bundle as secure as possible. After that, he sat down with his bowie knife and the sheets off the bed. He began slicing the sheets into two-inch wide strips of cloth like bandages, which he tied together to make a thin rope. They were on the third floor, and the old building had high ceilings, so he calculated he would need at least seventy, perhaps eighty feet of the lightweight linen rope to accomplish what he wanted.

Wolfe whistled a little under his breath as he worked, fashioning the rope. He smiled and stopped the whistling though, when he realized he was confusing the poor dog, which sat alertly by his side, tilting its head one way and then the other, trying to determine just what it was that the whistling signified.

Wolfe ruffled the animal's nape and scratched its ears. "Just hang in there, fella. I'll take you for a nice, long walk after a while."

CHAPTER SEVENTEEN

Wolfe awoke late in the afternoon, feeling edgy after a restless sleep. He was not worried so much about himself as about Becca. It was one thing to put his own life on the line, quite another to be responsible for hers. "What do you think, boy? You don't look worried." He scratched the dog just forward of its tail, a spot it seemed to particularly like, then both of them left the bed. Wolfe pulled on his clothing, and led the dog downstairs to the dining room. There were half a dozen diners already there, all of them young men wearing the now-familiar grey sweatshirts, jeans, and sneakers that were almost a uniform in Mistress Alethia's Paradise.

A rather homely, middle-aged woman was waiting on the tables. "We just got some beef in," she told him. "Would you like a steak?"

Steaks and roasts and ribs, he was used to, thanks to the deer and other game, including once-domesticated cattle gone feral since the war. But, what he really wanted… "Ma'am? Would it be possible to get a hamburger, do you think?"

The woman smiled. "It's surprising how many folks feel the same way. How many burgers would you like?"

"I can have more than one?"

"As many as you like."

"Three," he said promptly. "No, wait—make that…could I have five?"

"Five?"

He shrugged. "Two for the dog, three for the glutton—it's been… it has been a very long time."

"Sit and enjoy your coffee. I'll bring you five hamburgers as quickly as I can."

Wolfe could scarcely believe his good fortune. But he was not pleased enough about it to consider staying here in Paradise. The price of a hamburger was simply too high around here if it meant accepting the idea of theft and bullying and murder. That would not, however, stop him from enjoying the treat of a real hamburger served with ketchup and a dill pickle. "Hold the condiments for the dog's portion."

CHAPTER EIGHTEEN

Wolfe turned off the light and paused for a moment to marvel at how easily he had readjusted to having electric lights after he arrived in Paradise. He moved to the window and raised the sash. He was just leaning out to look around when he heard a knock on the door.

Grateful the visit had not occurred a few minutes later, he crossed the room and turned the bolt, then pulled the door open.

"Yes?"

Two young men stood there. One of them wearing the usual grey sweatshirt, but the other dressed rather nattily in tanned slacks and a forest green polo shirt. That one looked like his day job could have been as a junior executive in a multi-national company.

"May we come in?"

Wolfe stepped back and allowed them to enter. The seating choices were limited. There was one straight-backed chair, and the edge of the bed. Mr. Junior Exec helped himself to the chair without waiting for an invitation. The other remained standing beside the door with his arms folded.

Wolfe had the impression he might be there as some sort of guard, although that seemed to make no sense. Whatever these two wanted, Wolfe was not going to be put on the defensive about it. He sat down on the bed and waited for them to start the proceedings.

"My name is Calvin," the junior executive announced. "Your name is Wolfe, with an 'e'."

Wolfe could not remember if he'd given his name to the two men who brought him here, perhaps he had. He just didn't remember.

"The leader's abilities continue to amaze," Calvin said. "She named you Wolf without knowing your true name. Somehow, she discerned the truth. The leader is worthy, don't you think?"

"The leader is quite something," Wolfe agreed. "Very special," he said. Silently, to himself, he added, *She is also very vicious, cruel, and arrogant.* But she was quite something, indeed. It was just that he and Calvin had rather different reasons to think of her as being something special.

"You are a wanted man," Calvin said. "You should understand that we have no reason to care what the Federal Command wants of you. You are beyond their influence while you remain here with us. I suspect you already gathered as much."

"Yes, I did," Wolfe told him.

"On the other hand, the leader could turn a handsome profit by selling you to, erm…" Calvin dug in his shirt pocket for a scrap of paper. "To a certain…Ralph."

"Alston," Wolfe provided for him. "Ralph, and his ugly brother, Ed."

"Alston. How do you spell that?"

Wolfe gave Calvin his best guess. He hadn't had occasion to see the brothers' name in writing.

Calvin took a ball point pen out of his pocket and wrote it down. "Thank you. The leader was not sure about that."

"Funny, I would have thought she would have been able to discern it," Wolfe said.

"Do not take the leader lightly," Calvin warned. "This is very serious."

"Yes, I suppose it is."

"This Ralph Alston," Calvin went on, "has offered a substantial amount for you."

"Really?"

"Substantial." Calvin affirmed. "He wants you brought to him alive. There is a reward if you are dead, as well, but that would be considerably smaller."

Wolfe smiled. "The boys want the pleasure of doing things slowly," he said. "And I should think painfully, as well."

"That would not be the leader's concern," Calvin said.

"No, I suppose not."

"Do you mind if we turned the light on? It is almost dark."

"Go ahead," Wolfe said.

Calvin nodded, and the other man, the one by the door, flipped the switch to turn the overhead light back on. "The leader's question, Mr. Wolfe, is why should she allow you the privileges of residence here? Do you have any particular skills that would justify her turning down the payment offered by the Alston brothers, and are you willing to pledge your loyalty to the leader?"

"Well," Wolfe said, "I would have to admit that I don't have any special skills, none that I can think of. As for allowing myself to become one of your leader's goons, no, I'm not at all interested, thank you."

"Do you realize what you're saying, Mr. Wolfe?" Calvin asked.

"Oh, I kinda think that I do."

"In that case, Mr. Wolfe, James and I shall have to take you into custody. We will make you as comfortable as we can until the Alstons arrive to complete the purchase. Reasonably comfortable, in any event." Calvin smiled. "You may be glad to know that the leader had already determined that you are not one of the Regulators. If you had been, you would have been shot, regardless of any offer of payment the Alstons might make."

"Gee, I'm glad to know I don't have to worry about that."

"You don't sound as if you're taking this very seriously, Mr. Wolfe." Calvin chided him. "James and I will take you into custody now, if you please."

"And, if I don't please?"

"James and I are both highly skilled in the martial arts."

"I don't know anything about that stuff," Wolfe said.

"I really hope you will be cooperative about this. We have nothing against you personally, and we will not harm you unless you force us to. Will you come with us willingly, Mr. Wolfe?"

Wolfe stood, and so did Calvin. Wolfe grinned. "I reckon we'll just have to do this the hard way, sonny boy."

The two young karate experts growled and mumbled and made flashy movements with their hands. Silly-looking twits when they did that, Wolfe thought. He stood there and waited for them to come to him.

CHAPTER NINETEEN

Calvin led the way, edging forward with his hands poised, right foot forward, everything balanced and coordinated and surely adhering to whatever book the stance came from.

If the man hadn't been so deadly serious about all this, Wolfe would have found it amusing. As it was, though, he had to take it with no small degree of caution. He did not know enough about the martial arts to have any idea what Calvin would do first. Wolfe's only experience with it consisted of watching some Jackie Chan movies, and some reruns of the old TV show, Kung Fu. Heck, he'd never even seen a Bruce Lee film.

Calvin was close now, and began weaving back and forth like a cobra in front of a snake charmer.

"Have you ever seen Bruce Lee?" Wolfe asked Calvin in a conversational tone of voice.

"What?!"

Wolfe hit him—hard. He used the heel of his palm so that he would not break his knuckles, and drove the punch straight from the shoulder, stepping into it with the weight of his body behind it.

The extraordinary strength he'd acquired inside that mine tunnel made his blow a deadly one. Calvin's head snapped back with such force that Wolfe could hear a distinctive snap as the neck and spinal column broke, and the handsome young man collapsed like a marionette with its strings cut.

Very likely, Calvin was dead before his body struck the floor. Wolfe turned to take on James, only to discover that he was in no immediate danger from that quarter.

The dog had leaped for James and the young man was lying on his back now with the dog standing over him. James lay with both arms wrapped protectively over his head; there was blood on his chin.

"What is it with you?" Wolfe asked the dog. "Are you deliberately going for the face? Or do you just have lousy aim when you jump at the throat?"

"Get him off me! Please? Please, mister!"

"Dog. Back off!"

The dog backed away and sat on its haunches, looking interested in what was happening here but not at all aggressive now that James was down and Wolfe had taken over.

Wolfe knelt beside James. He felt a deep sense of sadness. "You and your leader murder people," he said.

"No! Never. Execute," James said. "Sometimes. Only those who deserve it. Really." He took his arms away from his face. The dog bite was hardly more than a scratch and had stopped bleeding already.

"You were going to execute me, too."

"No. Calvin told you the truth. The leader knows you aren't a Regulator."

"You were going to sell me to the Alston brothers."

"I...the leader. Not me! Not us!" James rolled his head.

"Calvin…is he…is he dead?"

"Yes, he is."

"He was—you don't look that tough, Mr. Wolfe, or that fast." James shuddered. "We didn't know…" His voice trailed away.

Wolfe smiled. "If you had known, you would have brought guns, is that it?"

"No! Certainly not!"

"I guess we'll never know now, though, will we?"

"Look, I…can I sit up? Can we talk?"

"There really isn't any need for that," Wolfe told him. "But I want you to understand that you haven't given me much choice here."

"What do you mean, Mr. Wolfe?"

Wolfe reached down and placed one hand on either side of James' head. He twisted sharply. The neck broke with a loud pop of tearing cartilage and bone, and James was gone, too. Wolfe rolled the two bodies beneath the bed and rearranged the blanket so that it was draped off the side and halfway onto the floor. It was not a very thorough job, but would have to do.

"Ready, buddy?" he asked the dog. "I think it's time we got out of here, if you don't mind."

CHAPTER TWENTY

Wolfe got the rucksack out of the wardrobe and the rope he'd made by cutting up the sheet. He threaded one end of the linen rope through a shoulder strap on the ruck and pulled it so that the rope was doubled.

He pushed the window screen out at the bottom and looked around outside the building with care. He'd hoped to wait until later when it would be completely dark and there were not apt to be any people moving around, but he did not think that he had that much time now. Sooner or later, someone was bound to come searching for Calvin and James, and once those two were found, these people would be using guns, not karate.

Using the homemade rope, he lowered the rucksack into the bushes growing in a tangle at the side of the old hotel, then let go of one end, so he could pull the cord through the shoulder strap and retrieve it. He certainly could not leave it dangling from the third-floor window, and if he simply dropped it, the light linen would end up draped over a bush like a white flag waving in the night.

He wadded up the rope and tossed it under the bed with

the two bodies and then snapped the overhead light off. He wondered as he did so if that was the last time he'd ever have the use of electric lights, for surely there could not be many enclaves in the country like this one fashioned by Mistress Alethia, with her flaming red hair and utter lack of morals.

"Come on, boy." Wolfe patted his thigh and the dog came tail-wagging to his side. They went downstairs and into the lobby.

"Where are Calvin and James?"

Wolfe did not recognize the man who sat in one of the aging armchairs. He was prepared for such a question, though. "They're upstairs waiting for me. The dog has to go out. I won't be long."

The man nodded and went back to the tattered magazine he'd been reading.

Wolfe pushed his goggles down to his throat and took a deep breath, savoring the fresh, clean air, and sense of freedom that came from no longer having an elastic band tied around his head. This early in the evening, he could see as well as if it were high noon. Later, in the darkest part of the night, it would seem to him like an overcast day.

"This way," he murmured to the dog. He went quickly around to the side of the hotel to the bushes where he'd dropped the rucksack, retrieved it, and pulled it on. Using the alleys so that he could avoid being spotted on the street, he headed at a swift trot for the motel that had been turned into the Paradise brothel, and the door of number '3'. The night before, Becca had said the girls were never moved around. She had no clothing, and was required to live and work in the one small room with food brought in twice a day. She had to 'entertain'—her word, not his—whoever the leader sent to her and occasionally, as with Wolfe, she had to pump them for information. One way or another, Wolfe figured, all of that was at an end.

He tapped lightly on her door and waited, then tapped it again, louder this time.

"Go away!" It was a man's voice inside, muffled, distorted by the closed door. Wolfe knocked again, louder this time, demanding.

"Open up! I have to look inside!"

"I'm telling you—"

There was a pause, and Wolfe very faintly heard what he supposed was Becca's voice. A moment later, he heard the rattle of a chain and the turning of the deadbolt. The door was snatched open, and a very angry middle-aged man glared at him. The man was naked, quite hairy, too, with bowed legs and a pot belly. His hairline was receding toward eventual baldness, if the man lived long enough for that to happen.

Wolfe had to push the man backward in order to step into the room.

"Hey! You can't do that!"

"I'm here, aren't I?"

"But—"

Wolfe clipped him on the jaw with a short, left hook. He tried to pull the punch; even so, he was afraid he'd hit the man too hard and perhaps done permanent damage. All he wanted to do was knock the fellow out, and he'd certainly done that. Becca was on the bed. She looked embarrassed.

"Are you all right?" He asked. He took the rucksack off and dropped it beside the bed.

Becca nodded. "Is he…you didn't kill him or anything, did you?"

"No, at least I don't think I did. He seems to be breathing. Do you have running water here?"

"What a strange question!" she asked.

"Maybe so, but do you have water in the bathroom? Did they hook up the pipes to here?"

"Sure. All over town, mostly. They just tied the windmills into the old water system."

"Good."

Wolfe yanked the sheet off the bed and took it into the rather grubby, old-fashioned little bathroom. He ran the basin full of water and dunked the sheet into it, moving it under the faucet until the thin material was thoroughly soaked.

"What are you doing?"

He grinned. "Tying up our guest in there."

"With a sheet?"

"A soaking wet sheet. I'll spread it out on the floor, put him on it, and then roll it nice and snug around him. The sheet will stick to itself as tight as tape. He won't be able to move a muscle until the cloth dries. By then, you and I will be long gone."

"That's neat. Will it really work?"

The grin returned. "We better hope so. I've never actually done this, you understand, but I read about it in a book once."

Becca rolled her eyes.

"While I finish this, you'll find a sweatshirt and jeans and socks in the top of the ruck there. No choice of size, I'm afraid. The only spare shoes I have are my old ones. Or you can take his if they'll fit you better. Anyway, get yourself dressed, girl. You and I have some serious hiking to do."

"I can't believe you really came back for me."

"I told you I would, didn't I?"

Becca did not say anything, but he could see the gratitude and the worry in her eyes before she turned and began digging clothing out of the rucksack.

Wolfe took the now thoroughly soaked sheet into the bedroom and quickly, but very carefully rolled the unconscious gent into it. He stuffed a washcloth into the man's mouth, and secured it in place with strips torn off the pillow-case. Gagging an unconscious man was dangerous; if he choked or threw up in response to the intrusion, he would drown in his own vomit. On the other hand, it would be much better for this guy to drown than for hooligans with guns to catch up with Wolfe and the girl.

It only took a few minutes before they were ready. Rebecca looked silly in the oversized clothes. In the old movies, Doris Day always managed to look cute and cuddly in Rock Hudson's white shirts. Funny thing, but real life was not turning out to be anything like that.

"Ready?"

"Yes, I—"

There was a loud bang and the room door was shoved violently open. Outside was the muscle-bound beach boy who tended the keys to the Paradise love nest. Blondie—Wolfe seemed to recall that his name was Andrew—looked peeved, and all the more so when he saw he was about to lose one of his charges. Andrew balled his massive hands into fists and stomped forward.

CHAPTER TWENTY-ONE

"Friend, you really don't want to do this," Wolfe said in a calm, reasonable tone. "Let me tie you up and I won't have to hurt you. Please."

Andrew gave the much-smaller, white-haired man an incredulous look and then laughed. "You? You think you can hurt me?"

"I don't want to. Let us go and I won't have to," Wolfe said.

"Old man! I'm gonna bust you up so bad they'll have to carry you out to the dump!"

Wolfe sighed. "I did try. I want you to remember that, Andrew. I tried."

The powerfully-built brothel keeper rolled his shoulders, showing off the slabs of bulging muscle there. He paused for a moment to give Wolfe time to see, and become frightened. Wolfe suspected that was a technique that worked very well, usually. This time—well…it had been worth a try even if it failed. Wolfe stood calmly waiting.

Andrew, the muscle-bound weightlifter, would not be the same sort of karate jock Calvin had been. He was very likely to—and there it came, just as expected. Andrew drew his powerful fist back and launched it toward Wolfe's jaw. Had it connected, it surely would have knocked Wolfe off his feet and very probably rendered him unconscious. Had it connected, that is. Wolfe swayed very slightly to the side then reached up and caught Andrew's balled fist in the palm of his own hand. Sort of like snagging a hot line drive drilled straight at an infielder's head. Wolfe caught the fist, then squeezed—hard. There was a rippling crunch, like kernels of popcorn all popping at once as the many tiny bones in the hand began to shatter. Andrew's face went suddenly pale beneath his tan. His jaw became slack. Then he screamed, the sound torn from his throat. He went to his knees and beads of cold sweat rolled off his forehead. Wolfe had to give the big man credit; Andrew was no quitter. He shook his head in an attempt to shake off his agony, then struggled to his feet. He cradled his broken right hand against his chest and turned to put his left shoulder forward. Despite the pain that had to be tearing him apart, he once again came forward, but this time at a very cautious shuffle instead of with the confident stride he'd shown before.

"Don't do this, Andrew. I swear, I don't want to hurt you anymore. Let me tie you up, please."

Andrew's response was so coarsely vulgar that Wolfe found himself embarrassed that Becca was in the room to hear it. This time, Andrew knew better than to begin his assault with a punch thrown straight from the shoulder. This time, he feigned the punch and instead tried to kick Wolfe in the crotch. Wolfe caught the man's foot on his thigh and stood poised, ready to clip Andrew with a hard right, even though his blow would almost surely break the man's neck and kill him. That was not necessary.

Rebecca stepped in behind Andrew and whacked him hard over the head with a heavy pottery water pitcher. The pitcher, Mexican or possibly Indian, judging by the design on it, cracked but did not shatter. "Tough stuff," Wolfe thought.

Andrew staggered backward on rubber legs, then dropped to his knees. Becca hit him again. This time, the pitcher broke apart. Andrew's eyes rolled up so only the whites of his eyeballs could be seen, and he toppled forward.

"I didn't kill him, did I?"

"No, but he's going to have one heck of a headache when he wakes up," Wolfe said, smiling at her. "Thanks."

Becca grinned. "Should I soak the other sheet now?"

"Yeah. Then you and I will be on our way. Uh, do you mind if I have another of those soft drinks before we go?"

"Take all you can carry." She pulled the bottom sheet off the bed and took it into the bathroom, where soon Wolfe could hear the water running. Lordy, but it was nice to have civilized comforts again, like electric lights and running water. And hamburgers...oh, my...hamburgers! Wolfe sighed. He would miss those things.

He would not miss much of anything else about Paradise, though. He set about looking for something he could use to gag Andrew before they made their break for freedom.

CHAPTER TWENTY-TWO

"Slow down! I can't see where we're going," Rebecca whispered.

"It's okay. I can see just fine. Hold onto my arm. If you stumble, I'll catch you."

"Can we stop for a minute so I can catch my breath?"

"You're in awful shape. Do you know that?"

"Yeah. Well, it was kind of hard to put my ten miles in each morning inside that room."

"I hadn't thought of that." He did relent, slowing to a walk, and then after a moment, coming to a halt.

Becca bent over and braced her hands on her knees as she gasped for breath. They had only been on the move for twenty minutes or so and had not yet gotten past all of the Paradise guards. Wolfe could still see a road block ahead, and what he thought was another outpost on top of a bluff to the south of the county blacktop that ran through what used to be a perfectly nice town called Tifton.

Wolfe gave Becca a moment to catch her breath, and then asked, "Do you happen to know where those Regulators are?"

"I think so. I think they're in Delaney."

"Sorry, that isn't telling me anything."

She straightened up and bent backward, then to either side, loosening up.

"Feel better?" he asked.

"Yes, thanks."

"And Delaney is…?" he prompted.

"It's a town, or was. It's even smaller than Tifton. It's about fifteen miles down this road. Is that where we're going?"

He nodded, then remembered that her night vision was not as clear as his own. "Yes, I think so."

"Why?"

"Ever hear of the old saying, "The enemy of my enemy is my friend?"

"Sure, but I never believed it."

"Even so, I have a score to settle with Mistress Alethia and her idiot followers. They were going to sell me to my enemies, or kill me. If we can do anything that will help those Regulators, give them information or whatever, then I think we ought to. Besides, I have to take you someplace. Is there anywhere other than Delaney you'd like to go?"

"I've always thought Hawaii sounded nice," she said with a grin.

"I'll see what I can do. In the meantime, Delaney."

"Can't we rest for just a minute more?" she asked.

"No. Fifteen miles, you said? That's a four-hour walk, and I want to get there early enough that I can get a look around before daylight. I don't want any more of the surprises like what I ran into back there in Paradise."

"You're a hard man to get along with, Jim Wolfe."

"Yeah, but I'm cute. It's the only thing that saved me."

"You know, for such an old guy, you really are kind of cute," Becca ran in place for a second or two, then did some high knee lifts to warm up and get her legs limber again. "All right. I suppose I'm ready whenever you are."

Wolfe strode out, angling away from the blacktop so they could swing well away from the roadblock that lay ahead. Mistress Alethia's thugs would be armed with rifles, and he did not want to take them on with only his bow and bowie knife.

CHAPTER TWENTY-THREE

Delaney looked like a ghost town. It was, or had been, a crossroads with a gas station, a small hardware store, a café, and a dozen or so frame homes. Wolfe parked Becca in the backseat of an old, abandoned Plymouth minivan and crept forward alone. If there were Regulators around, they hadn't posted any guards or set up any defenses against Mistress Alethia and her minions.

Minions, Wolfe thought, with an amused half smile. He never met a minion before he came to Paradise. Now, he had met several of them. He became more sober. Killed some, too. He hated that, but did not see that he really had any choice in the matter—not if he wanted to keep on living himself. And, as long as there was the slightest shred of hope that Lurleen and Jojo might still live, he intended to remain alive to find them.

He made a slow circle around the tiny town of Delaney, then silently passed by several of the outlying houses and approached the building that had been a gas station. Signs still in place showed that the station also offered snacks, sodas, small engine repairs. Now there was an appetizing combination.

The gas station seemed to have been abandoned. So did the café next door. Although, the café door was closed and locked, blinds drawn down over the glass at the windows and the front door.

"Hello?" Wolfe called softly. "Is anyone here?"

There was no response. Not that he really expected one. He walked more quickly and openly this time out the road leading to the east, and tapped on the side window of the Plymouth. "Becca, you can come out now."

There was no response. Probably fell asleep, he guessed. She would be tired after walking fifteen miles. He went around to the other side of the minivan and pulled the sliding door open. "Becca, wake up. It's okay. Wake up and come out now."

When there was still no answer, Wolfe stuck his head inside the rusting Plymouth. "Rebecca?"

He heard a thin, high-pitched squeak. Then the twin muzzles of a double-barrel shotgun touched the side of his face.

"Don't move."

The instruction was entirely superfluous. Wolfe had no intention of challenging a double-barrel scattergun at point blank range. Not on his life.

CHAPTER TWENTY-FOUR

They held Wolfe in what had been a storage room at the back of the gas station. He was not tied up, but he'd had to deposit the rucksack in the front room beside a useless cash register. And one of the men—there were three of them—asked him very politely for the bowie. Wolfe looked at the shotgun first, then meekly handed over the big knife.

They hadn't searched him and he still had a folding lock blade knife in his pocket, but had no illusions about over-coming all odds with just that for a weapon. The dog really did not count in the weapon category, he decided, leaning down to ruffle its fur and scratch behind its ears.

Becca had been taken elsewhere by the Regulators; at least, he assumed these were some of the dreaded Regulators. Dreaded, that is, by the people of Paradise. So far, Wolfe could not see that there was all that much difference between them, except that the Regulators seemed to be older and not so well-dressed. Everyone in Paradise wore the uniform grey sweatshirts and blue jeans. The men in Delaney dressed like any country folk might. He hoped they behaved better than the ones in Paradise, though. He would hate to take Becca out of one sort of ill treatment just to deposit her into another.

Time passed slowly inside the windowless storage room, and there was no place to sit. Eventually, he sat cross-legged in a corner. The dog curled up at his side with its head in his lap; Wolfe closed his eyes.

He roused to the sound of a padlock rattling at the door, and a moment later, the room was flooded with light. The sun must have come up while he was imprisoned—detained would be a nicer way to put it—and the sudden light made him wince in pain. He quickly slipped the welding goggles in place and felt immediately and immensely better.

"You can come out now. Sorry, but we had to make sure of you, Mr. Wolfe."

Obviously, these people had been talking with Rebecca.

"My name is Adams," the man said, extending his hand. "Bill Adams, or the Reverend William F. Adams, if you want to get formal about it."

Adams was probably fifty or so, with bushy eyebrows and a very bad haircut. He wore shorts, a t-shirt, and Mexican peasant-style sandals that had been cut from a used tire. The sandals were not elegant, but they would do the job, and God knew there were more than enough truck and car tires lying about. Adams did not look like a pre-war preacher, but then, these were odd times and civilization had not yet adjusted to the world's many changes.

"You used to be a preacher?" Wolfe asked.

"Not 'used to be.'" Adams corrected. "I still am. If anything, these external circumstances have only served to strengthen my calling."

"Are you the leader of the Regulators?" Wolfe asked.

Adams laughed. "There are no Regulators, Mr. Wolfe. Not to our minds, anyway. That is a name applied by our 'neighbors' so they can lump us together and view us as an enemy, or so I assume. Their leader, that woman—how shall I put this?—she is delusional. I mean that. She has visions of leading an empire. A small one, but an empire nonetheless. And I'm afraid in doing so she has become a very bad neighbor, indeed."

"I can certainly agree with that." Wolfe said.

Adams motioned for him to come out of the storage room. "Your things are where you put them. You can reclaim them whenever you wish."

The rucksack looked untouched; Wolfe left it there. He did, however, retrieve the big bowie knife from the store counter where someone had put it. He felt a little better with that at his belt again.

"Come with me, please." Adams led the way outside and then next door to the café. The blinds had been raised now and the door was unlocked. Rebecca was inside; so were more than a dozen men and women of varying ages and a handful of children who played in solemn silence at the back of the place. Wolfe joined Becca and took a chair at one of the café's dozen or so tables.

"Are you all right?"

She smiled. "Oh, yes. I know most of these people. Some of them used to live in Tifton, before—you know. Before she took over everything. They spoke up for me this morning. They already knew a lot of what goes on over there."

"They vouched for you and then you vouched for me, is that it?"

She nodded. "Yeah, kind of like that."

The residents of Delaney came filing past and Wolfe stood to greet them, shaking hands and immediately forgetting the names that went with the faces. The children, he saw, remained isolated at the back, and there were sounds coming from the kitchen that suggested there were more people here than he had seen so far. Not that he minded. Just as long as these were not more of Mistress Alethia's grey-shirted thugs, he was satisfied. When everyone present had introduced themselves, Bill Adams and another man joined Wolfe and Becca at the table.

"Becca has been filling us in on the plans to wipe us out," the second man said.

"I'm sorry, but what was your name again?"

"Tom Hardesty."

"Right, Tom. Did you say something about them wanting to wipe you out?"

"I'm not the one who said it." Hardesty nodded toward Rebecca. "She did."

Wolfe looked at her and raised an eyebrow.

"You didn't know?" she asked.

"No, I never heard anything about that."

"Well, I sure did. The men they sent to see me liked to talk about it. Some of them seemed really obsessed by the idea. They want to expand; bring windmills and pump the water from over here so they can raise more alfalfa and maybe some grain crops, oats, or milo. For the horses, you see. The leader says horses will be the base for nearly all wealth in the future."

"She may be right about that, too," Adams agreed. "She already has every horse that used to be in this county, and just about all the others around here, too. She had her people steal them: the horses, a few of the cattle, and every windmill they could spot. They came in with guns and took every-thing. Towers, mills, and all. Anyone who tried to stop them, they shot. Murdered is what I call it. They must have slaughtered upward of fifty people around here. That was before we learned we should all come together, so we could oppose them in numbers they would have to respect."

"They're like bullies anywhere," Hardesty added. "Once we presented a united front, they pulled back. We hoped that was the end of it."

"Have you tried to talk with them?" Wolfe asked.

"Once," the preacher said. "Walter never came back."

"He was executed," Becca said. "Out at the dump, where I told you. I know the one who shot him. Shot him in the back of the head. He was proud of himself for doing that, he said. The leader gave him four extra nights at the motel. He…" she hesitated and lowered both her eyes and voice. "He spent all of them with me. That's how I know."

Adams reached out and laid a comforting hand on Becca's wrist. Rebecca looked at the preacher and said, "Your friend's name was Walter Sensibaugh, right?"

"Yes, exactly."

The girl shuddered. "He was so proud of himself for doing what the leader wanted."

"That woman may have been proud, but God takes notice of these things, too. Whoever he is, he'll not escape punishment. Not in the long run."

"The hell with the long run," Hardesty said. "I'd like to see him get his comeuppance in this world."

Adams gave him a sorrowful look and Hardesty looked away, but he did not retract what he'd said and his anger was apparent.

"What about this plan of theirs to add Delaney to Alethia's empire?" Wolfe asked. "Do you know when they'll be coming? And just as important, do they have any reason to realize that you know so much?"

Becca shook her head. "No date has been set exactly.

They're waiting for the leader to give the order, the ones I talked with. Listened to, is more like it. They said they're ready to go at an hour's notice. That's all they knew. They said an hour's notice. At least three or four of them used that same term: 'hour's notice'."

"Did they say how they'll come?"

"In the wagons. That's probably why the hour's delay. They'll have to bring up all the wagons and enough horses to pull them, then get them all hitched. The men will get aboard the wagons and they will come down the road fast, with guns ready to cut right through Delaney and murder everyone here who won't give allegiance to the leader."

"Our allegiance is elsewhere," the preacher said softly. "That is not negotiable."

"Then you have to prepare to defend yourselves," Wolfe said.

Adams sighed. "We have perhaps a dozen shotguns, and a handful of pistols, and rifles and very little ammunition for any of them. I doubt that a military confrontation will serve us well, yet I see no other choice. We will have to defend the town from these people whenever they choose to come."

"Is there anyone here with military experience who could lead you? Police, retired Army or Marines, anyone like that at all?"

"No," Hardesty said. "Not one. Are you?"

"Sorry, I don't know any more than the stuff I've read in novels or seen in movies, but I don't know. Let's walk around and look things over. Maybe we can get some ideas."

"You will help us?"

Staying here and involving himself in a war between Mistress Alethia's Paradise thugs and the mild country folk of Delaney was a stupid, stupid thing for a stranger to do.

"Yes," Wolfe heard himself say. "I'll help if I can."

Rebecca took his hand and squeezed it. Adams turned to

Hardesty and said, "Get John and Andrew, please. They might have some thoughts to add, as well. Then we should all go and see if we can devise a war plan." He gave a small, rueful smile and added, "David was no warrior, either, yet he defeated the giant. Remind me to use that for the theme of my next sermon, will you?"

CHAPTER TWENTY-FIVE

"Entrapment," Wolfe mused aloud.

"What was that you said?"

"Nothing, really, I… I was just—it's silly of me, really."

"Please. Tell us," the preacher insisted.

"Yeah, well, I was thinking about a movie I saw once. I don't remember what movie it was—some old western on TV—I guess I thought about it because Becca said the Paradise army will be coming in horse-drawn wagons, and it kind of…it kind of fit, if you see what I mean."

Adams smiled. "No, I can't say that I do understand quite yet. Go on."

"Well, you see, over on this west end of town, there's only the main street, the state highway or whatever it is. No side streets or anything until you get to that north-south highway over there. There are those dirt streets that run parallel to the east-west highway, and there's the cross streets over on the east side of town past that road. But over on this end, there's only the one road and it's about—what, three blocks long? Or would be, if there were any cross streets to measure by."

"Somethin' like that, yes."

"So, what I was thinking; you could block the alleys between the buildings around here—put up barricades, sort of, but you'd want to build them so they didn't look like barricades. And that is where you'd want to put your fighters, in there behind the barricades. Then, after that—are you sure you want to listen to all this? I'm probably just being silly here, thinking about some old movie that I don't even remember the name of."

Adams smiled. "You are not being silly, and I do want to hear what you have to say. Mind, now, we might not take your advice, but we do want to hear it."

"If you're sure, then," Wolfe took a deep breath and went on with the idea that he'd gotten from that movie. Darn, he wished he could remember what it had been, or even who starred in it. Audie Murphy, maybe. He really liked Audie Murphy. Now there was a fighter. They could use him, or somebody like him, here in Delaney.

CHAPTER TWENTY-SIX

"I'm sorry we have so little food to offer," Reverend Adams apologized. They were gathered in the former café where there were enough tables and chairs to accommodate everyone. "We are out of very nearly everything."

The meal consisted of a sort of multi-hued mush that might have been made from almost anything. It tasted like almost nothing. Its only virtues were that it was hot and filling.

"I thought I saw some grain crops outside town," Wolfe said.

"More of a failing experiment than a crop, I'm afraid. We planted oats, barley, and corn this spring. The corn barely broke the surface before it withered and died. The oats were in the ground too late to do any good, or so I'm told. What you saw was the barley, and our farmers tell me they doubt the barley will make any yield to speak of."

"Why's that?" Rebecca asked. "It can't be the weather or the soil. In Paradise, they're able to grow grains."

"Water," Adams said. "We have wells, of course, from before civilization died. Some of the shallow wells still have mill towers, but the people over there came and took the windmills. If we had even a few of those mills back, we could pump enough water to irrigate a little land, grow some garden crops and have a community well for drinking and washing. As it is, we've jury-rigged some cisterns, but now even those are low, and we aren't expecting any more rain until fall. We are thinking about trying to devise some sort of snow collection for winter. Really, though, many of us are beginning to believe we'll not be able to hold out here much longer. If those people in Tifton—excuse me, please, but I can't bring myself to think of it as Paradise. For me, that has a very different meaning than what those people offer. If they were smart, they would simply wait until next spring or so. We would all be forced to leave and they could take over Delaney without opposition, once it becomes a ghost town like all the others around here."

"What happened to the people in all those places?" Wolfe asked.

"They walked away. Some said they would be going east where the Federal Command would take care of them, a few said they'd go to Canada or Mexico. How many of them survived and where they've gone, we just don't know."

"So Delaney will die, too?" Wolfe asked.

"Very likely."

"Then why bother to oppose Alethia's people at all? You could just give in to them, negotiate surrender terms, perhaps get them to outfit your people with food and water enough that they can reach the clear area, and turn themselves in to FEDCOM for help."

"This is our home, Mr. Wolfe," the preacher said. "We may be forced out of it, but we'll not go willingly." His expression hardened and he lifted his chin defiantly. "We'll not go at the point of any man's gun."

Wolfe nodded. It was an attitude he could respect. "If you

don't mind, I'd like to find a place where I can get some sleep. We had a long night last night and a longer day today."

Adams turned and motioned for a boy of perhaps twelve or thirteen to leave his seat and come to their table. The boy's skin was loose and very slightly wrinkled. It took Wolfe a moment to realize why. He had been a plump child before the war. Now, all traces of baby fat were gone. Much longer, and he would look positively gaunt.

"Billy, I'd like you to take Mr. Wolfe down to Mrs. Wilcox's house. No one's living there, but I noticed the other day the door's open. He can sleep there, I think." To Wolfe he added, "Make yourself at home there, Mr. Wolfe. I don't know what condition the bedding will be in, but at least you'll be inside in the shade and no one will bother you there."

"All right. Thank you," he said.

"I want to stay here and visit a little longer," Becca said. "There are some old friends I'd like to catch up with."

Wolfe had not expected her to accompany him to begin with, although apparently she felt some obligation to do so.

"I'll see all of you later on, then," he said. He bent to pick up his rucksack and turned to the boy. "Lead on, Billy. I'll be right behind you."

CHAPTER TWENTY-SEVEN

The house was small, an aging frame structure that looked like it might have been built in the 1930's. There were tangles of weeds and dried up flower plants in beds across the front of the tiny yard and in front of the porch. A rocking chair sat to one side of the front door. A screen door with a ragged tear in the metal screen fabric stood very slightly ajar. The wooden door behind was open.

Wolfe felt a sadness looking at the house and thinking about what had been before and never would be again.

"Was the owner of the house one of those who went away after the war?"

"No, sir, Mrs. Wilcox died. She had the sugar diabetes, and after the war she couldn't get no more, um…no more of the medicine she needed."

"Insulin?"

"Yeah, somethin' like that, anyway."

It hadn't occurred to Wolfe before, but people all over the country who were dependent upon medications would have found themselves without the prescriptions they took so casually for granted. Took for granted until that day when artificial suns flashed in so many places, that is. After that, a great many of them must have succumb to their diseases.

"Thanks for showing me the way," Wolfe said.

"Can I ask you somethin', mister?"

"Sure."

"Is there…I mean, you been over there, you seen those people. Are they like everybody says? A-are they gonna come here and kill us?"

Wolfe laid a hand on the boy's shoulder. "We are going to see if we can't keep them from doing that, Billy."

"I guess…" The kid turned his head away and stared off into the distance. "I guess when you think about it, it don't make much difference if they do or they don't."

Wolfe shuddered. What a horrible thing for a little boy to feel.

"We'll all do what we can, son. We'll do our very best."

"Yes, sir," the boy said, his voice empty of hope.

He turned and walked away, leaving Wolfe to find his own way indoors.

CHAPTER TWENTY-EIGHT

The inside of the house was almost as dreary as its exterior. There was one great difference Wolfe saw between this little place, though, and all those he'd come across since he'd walked out of that mine tunnel into a world that was upside down: this house had been searched and emptied of all that was valuable—that was only to be expected—but here, there was no vandalism. Elsewhere, it looked like the roving bands of brigands, wanderers and vagabonds picked through the contents of abandoned properties with deliberately malicious intent. Drawers were not simply opened. They were yanked out and spilled onto the floor. Closets were not investigated. They were emptied, with their contents strewn about the room. Beds were stripped of their sheets, mattresses overturned in the hope of finding something, anything, hidden there.

In this tidy little house, the neighbors who came to pick through Mrs. Wilcox's belongings did so with a modicum of respect, perhaps even with love for the departed lady. Wolfe liked that. It spoke well of the people of Delaney.

He looked into the kitchen and the pantry. There was

absolutely no point in doing that; he did it anyway. You never knew. The only things still in the pantry were a box of toothpicks, and on the floor some cleaning products. Silver polish, Bon Ami, and a few jars with small amounts of dark liquid pooled in them—these could have been almost anything.

He knew better than to open the ancient refrigerator; he looked inside it anyway. The shelves were bare. The tiny freezer compartment held only a pair of dry, empty ice cube trays. There was a sour stink from an old spill of some unknown material.

There were curtains at the kitchen window. The window must once have looked out onto the backyard. Now, the view was of a dark room, a lean-to that had been tacked onto the house where a porch might originally have been. The added room held a daybed, a sewing machine, and a rack where a number of shapeless house dresses were hanging.

The living room was bright, with drapes pulled over the windows and a mountain of overstuffed pillows arranged on the sofa, and an upholstered easy chair. An old-fashioned television set with a rounded, fishbowl-type screen dominated one wall. Surrounding it were dozens of framed photographs: scrubbed children, picnic scenes, many of a pleasant-looking man. Some of the pictures of the man showed him as a very young soldier; others chronicled his aging.

"And then there were none," Wolfe said aloud.

He went into the one bedroom. The bed was a double, the mattress feather-soft. It might have been a genuine feather mattress, actually. There were braided rugs on the floor, an alarm clock on the bedside table. The clock, an electric model, was stopped at two-seventeen. The time of the nuclear explosions? He could not remember, and anyway, it would have been different bombs that disturbed things down here. Probably the ones that crippled Delaney were the ones targeted to Salt Lake City.

A clean and very lovely quilt was spread over the bed. Wolfe looked at it and very quickly decided he did not want to disturb the handmade quilt, nor anything else that was here. Not any more than he positively had to. Besides, this room was the brightest and the lightest in the house. If he went into the back and slept in the little add-on sewing room, he would be comfortable on the daybed and would be able to remove his goggles, as well.

He dropped his rucksack in the living room, this obviously a community where theft would not be a problem, and returned to the dark little lean-to so that he could get some badly-needed sleep. There was no telling when the men from Paradise would come. He wanted to be rested and ready to receive them whenever that proved to be. The dog agreed, jumping onto the daybed before Wolfe could secure his spot.

CHAPTER TWENTY-NINE

I t was not the men from Paradise who came for him. Rather, it was the men from Delaney.

Wolfe woke to find a half-dozen men crowded into or near the little lean-to where he was sleeping. He sat up, blinking, and pulled the dark goggles over his eyes. The door the men opened was emitting too much light for comfort.

"What is it? Are they coming?"

"Why don't you tell us?" A stalky, middle-aged man demanded.

Wolfe had met him earlier, but could not recall his name now. He was balding with a round, red-cheeked face. He did not look cherubic in the slightest, and the shotgun in his hand made a Santa Claus impression unlikely. Especially since the gun was pointed at Wolfe's chest.

"What's wrong?"

"Spy!" one of the others snapped, mouthing the word as if it were a curse.

"Traitor!" another one added.

"What the devil are you people talking about?" Wolfe asked, a little peevish himself after being dragged out of a sound sleep so he could listen to these rather silly accusations.

"Come with us." The bald man, his name was…it began with a 'C', Wolfe was fairly sure about that. Not Charlie, though. Carl? Casey? Kent! That was it. Not exactly a 'C', then, but the sound was close enough. Kent.

Kent took Wolfe by the upper arm and pulled. Just because he did not like the man's attitude, Wolfe resisted the tugging and braced himself. Kent might as well have been pulling on the wall of the house for all the good he accomplished.

"Would you care to tell me what's going on here?" Wolfe asked.

"You're a spy for them turkeys over in Tifton and we know it! We got you figured, mister. You come in here pretending to be our friend, you find out how many of us there are and what we're armed with. You even come up with a defensive plan that sounds good, except since you and that redhead both know what it is, you'll be proposing to us they will be ready for it. Just sweep right around and get behind us and then we're done for. Isn't that the way you planned it? Isn't it?!"

"Have you been smokin' somethin' funny, mister?" Wolfe asked. "You must have been to come up with somethin' like that. Smokin' that left-handed tobacco or maybe drinkin' Sterno? You're having hallucinations, whatever the cause."

"You're the one in trouble, here," Kent insisted. But he did not try to pull on Wolfe's arm again. "Now come along. The council wants to talk to you."

Wolfe sighed. He'd been enjoying the sleep. He really was, but it was shattered now, good and proper. Reluctantly, he stood up, yawned, and took time for a good stretch. None of the men from Delaney seemed to realize when he stretched his arms wide that he could have taken hold of a couple of them, and used their bodies to batter the others unconscious before any of them had time to react. Wolfe had not come here to commit mayhem, though. He merely wanted to help Rebecca and get a little back at Mistress Alethia and her bully boys. It was beginning to look, though, like these Delaney boys didn't want to play nice. If it was going to be like that, there was no reason why Wolfe wouldn't just pick up his toys, such as they were, and leave. He didn't owe these people anything.

He glanced at the dog, another danger these Delaney fellows didn't seem to recognize as a threat. The animal was beside the foot of the bed where Wolfe had been sleeping. It was in a crouch, the hair on the back of its neck standing stiffly upright. One menacing move toward Wolfe and the dog would be at somebody's throat.

"It's okay, boy." Wolfe bent and rubbed the dog's head. It relaxed and began to wag its tail. He straightened and gave the men a cold look. "You said something about the council?"

He shoved his way through them, the dog close on his heels, and led the way back to the café where the Delaney public gathering seemed to be held.

CHAPTER THIRTY

A group of men sat there in chairs arranged so there was one empty table facing them and a chair placed so that it faced the Delaney council. Bill Adams, the Reverend Adams, sat in the center, with Tom Hardesty beside him. An empty chair to Adams's left was quickly taken by the man whose name Wolfe thought was Kent.

There were no women in evidence, nor were there any sounds of children coming from the kitchen. He gathered this bunch was serious in their newfound belief that he meant them harm.

Wolfe sat in the chair that was so obviously intended for him. He sat with his hands on top of the table, fingers laced loosely together. He felt no inclination to make things any easier for them by asking questions or making accusations. This was their idea; they could start the ball rolling if and when they wished.

After a minute or so, Bill Adams cleared his throat. "We, um, we have some questions to put to you, Mr. Wolfe."

"All right."

"You say you were taken by Alethia's people, and subtly questioned to determine if you were spying for us?"

"That's right," Wolfe agreed. "You can ask Rebecca about that. I hadn't known what they were doing until she told me about it."

"And you say you were only passing through when you encountered some of the Paradise men, who took you with them and introduced you to their leader?"

"Correct again," Wolfe said. "It was somewhere north of Paradise where they found me. I was on my way down from the Federal Command station at the edge of the clear area up there."

"Where you are wanted for murder, among other things," Kent interjected, his voice sharp and accusing.

Wolfe nodded. "Among other things. That charge was trumped up by some renegades named Alston. They have their own personal reasons for wanting me taken. The FEDCOM wants me for a murder they genuinely believe I committed. It was the Alstons who did it, not me."

"These Alstons also have a reward posted for your capture. Is that correct?" Kent asked.

"News travels fast, even without telephones and radio, doesn't it?" Wolfe said.

"And I suppose you are innocent in these matters?"

"The killings I've done, and there have been several including two Alston brothers, were all done in self-defense. I would do the same things again if given the same choices."

"So you claim," Kent said. There was acid in his voice.

"That's right. So I do indeed claim," Wolfe responded.

"Ms. Morrison tells us you left a man alive in Paradise."

"Did she also tell you that I had to kill another one there?"

"We questioned her closely. She did not herself examine that man to ascertain that he was dead. The whole thing could have been done for show, just to convince her, and through her, convince us that you are what you claim to be. I find it very curious that you would have left a living enemy behind. One capable of raising an alarm and a pursuit when you could have avoided that danger by dispatching him."

Wolfe smiled. Not that there was any mirth in the expression. He shook his head.

"First you accuse me because I'm said to have killed people, now you accuse me because I didn't murder someone. Which is it to be, Mr. Kent? You can't have it both ways."

"My name is Laffrey. Kent Laffrey, and I suggest you speak respectfully to this council."

"Then I, sir, suggest you earn respect. So far, I don't see any reason to give you any."

"Reverend!" Laffrey complained. "This man is not to be trusted. We cannot base our entire defense on ideas he's given us. I still feel that plan could well have been proposed by Alethia herself. Wolfe is only trying to carry out her desires, perhaps in an attempt to ingratiate himself to her. In any event, I think we should adopt the defense that I suggested to begin with."

"You people can come up with any plans that please you," Wolfe put in. "All I want to do is go home. This is all I've been trying to do ever since the war. Why don't I make us all happy and just walk away from here? You folks can fight it out with that Paradise crowd however you damn well please."

"Let you go?" Kent Laffrey said. "What, so you can run back to your leader and tell her she can't expect us to be lined up in the alleys along Main Street, ready for her killers to pick off from behind? Give you time to warn her so she can prepare a whole new plan to murder us all? I don't think so, Mr. Wolfe. I really do not think we would be so stupid as to do that!"

Wolfe sighed. "Mister, I tried to help out. But to tell you the truth, at this point, I don't care what happens to any of you. Not this Delaney crowd and certainly not those killers over in Paradise."

"We will need to consider everything that has been said here," Reverend Adams said. "We need time to do that. I think it would be best, Mr. Wolfe, if you were to remain in isolation until we reach our conclusions."

"In jail, you mean."

"We have no jail here."

"In isolation, then," Wolfe corrected himself.

"Isolation," Adams repeated. "Yes, that is a rather pleasant way to put it. Would you be willing to do that?"

"Or would you rather we blow your head off now instead of later?" Laffrey snarled.

"Let me guess," Wolfe said, looking calmly into Laffrey's eyes. "Diplomacy isn't your strong suit, is it?"

"Please cooperate," Adams said. "No harm will come to you, you have my word on that."

"I believe you are a man of your word, sir, but will your hot-headed friend honor your word, too?"

"Kent?"

Laffrey hesitated for a moment, then dropped his eyes. "All right, Bill. You've made a promise on behalf of the council. I won't be the one to break it." He glared at Wolfe. "But if he tries anything, we will shoot to kill. I want that understood."

Wolfe stood. He did not wait to be herded away like a criminal. He knew good and well he would be going back to that gas station supply room next door. And on the positive side of things, maybe he could finish that good sleep Laffrey and his frightened friends interrupted a little while earlier.

CHAPTER THIRTY-ONE

It was a good hour past dark before he heard voices outside his door. A moment later, there was the sound of a bolt being withdrawn, and Becca came in carrying a basket and a candle burning in a hurricane lamp. Just outside, Wolfe could see a guard seated on a lawn chair. He held a shotgun across his lap. Becca set the lamp on a shelf, and closed the door behind her.

"I'm sorry. I tried to tell them, but Mr. Laffrey wouldn't listen to me. Why would they do something like that? Why?"

Wolfe shrugged. "I don't suppose it really matters why. If I had to guess, I'd say the real cause is jealousy. Laffrey has some plan of his own. A stranger coming along with a different idea, especially a better idea, makes him look foolish, or anyway, makes him think others will believe him to be foolish. He wouldn't want to allow that. Heck, this could be the first time in his life he's ever been in a position where people listen to him. Now he's on the council, taking charge, defending the town, people looking up to him, and some stranger tries to minimize what he's done." Wolfe sighed. "I doubt that it has anything to do with me, really. I suspect it's a matter of Laffrey and an easily-bruised ego."

"I want you to know I really did try."

"I believe you."

"They will let you out once the danger's over. I'm sure of that."

Wolfe snorted. "Becca, judging from what I've seen so far, the danger will be over when the Paradise crowd either kills or captures all the people in Delaney. They will keep the ones they want and execute the rest, just like they did in Tifton. If that happens, girl, you will be back where you were, or worse. There's no telling what that woman might do to you by way of punishment for having fled her version of Paradise. And, of course, they will kill me on the spot and sell my corpse to the Alstons for whatever they can get, or mess me up and sell me to the Alstons still living. To tell you the truth, I think I'd rather end it here than go through whatever fun and games Ralph and Ed would come up with."

Becca shuddered. "I'm so very, very sorry."

"Not your fault. Not at all." He motioned toward the basket. "I don't suppose you brought me a file baked into a cake there, or a spoon I can use to tunnel my way out of here?"

"Nothing so dramatic, I'm afraid. Just a can of pork and beans."

"The real thing?"

"Yes, pre-war!"

He smiled. "Sounds like the best offer I've had all day."

"They made me open the can before I came in here. I hope you don't mind."

"Heaven forbid I should have any sharp objects." He laughed and pointed to the big bowie knife on his belt. No one had thought to take it from him, and he certainly was not going to suggest such a thing.

He accepted the can from Becca and poured half of it on the floor for the dog. Then, lacking a spoon or any other utensils, dipped the can up and drank the contents. The beans, swimming in a thin, sweet sauce, tasted wonderful.

"Could you do me a favor?" he asked between bites.

"If I can, certainly."

"The dog needs to go outside to do his business. Then bring him back, if you wouldn't mind." Wolfe smiled. "He's good company. Better than a lot of people I could think of."

"Do you have a leash for him?"

"No, but I imagine he'll go with you."

Becca snapped her fingers and patted her thigh. The dog gave Wolfe an inquiring look and only consented to go when Wolfe motioned toward the door.

Becca was back in five or six minutes. She let the dog back into the makeshift cell, returned the empty bean can to her basket, and took out a plastic soda bottle.

"Don't believe the label. It's only water."

"Water's fine, thanks."

She retrieved the candle and paused at the door to look back at him for a moment, then she was gone. He heard the sound of the bolt being closed again, locking him and the dog inside.

CHAPTER THIRTY-TWO

He spent the next two days in the cell. Becca came by several times each day, bringing him food and walking the dog while Wolfe ate. He enjoyed those breaks, but was not lonely during the times when he was alone. After years driving the highways alone in the cab of a truck plus two years alone in the bottom of the mine, he was accustomed to being by himself, and truth was, he found himself to be pretty good company.

He sang; Wolfe could not remember the words to very many songs, but he remembered long phrases and sometimes whole verses. He would sing those over and over again, and nearly always in the same voice as whichever artist recorded the piece. The thing was that Jim Wolfe had a singing voice that would have frightened women and terrified small children, so he sang without sound, and inside his head, his range was tremendous, his pitch, perfect. Why, sometimes, he could sing duets, or even sound exactly like Cher. On a good day, he could reproduce the entire Village People. As far as he was concerned, well, it was singing, sort of. And he enjoyed it.

On a not-so-good day, he spent his time thinking about Lurleen and Jojo. The memories were good ones: Lurleen in the kitchen, smiling and chattering, stopping in the middle of her work to pour him a fresh cup of coffee or walk over to him and give him a kiss behind the ear for no reason at all. Jojo, asleep with that stuffed pink elephant he adored, or the side-to-side way he used to run when he was barely able to walk, but refused to slow down in spite of that.

The memories would have been easier to bear if he only knew they were still alive. If he could be sure they were waiting for him. But then, they had to be, didn't they? Because if they were gone, then so was he. Breathing or walking, or lying cold and empty in a town dump, if Lurleen and Jojo were not alive, then neither was he. They had to be alive. Somewhere. And he had to find them. That was all there was to it. He had to return to them.

When those memories came to him, he sat on the storage room floor and pulled the dog into his lap and hugged it close, taking its warmth as a substitute for the comfort he really wanted to feel inside his arms. Singing inside his head was a far better way to pass the time. But he missed them. Good Lord, how he missed them. And if his eyes became moist at those times, well, he was probably coming down with a head cold or something like that.

It was on his third night confined in the makeshift jail cell that he heard the boom and crackle of gunfire nearby. The dog jumped to its feet, head tilted, ears erect. It looked at Wolfe and gave him a tentative and questioning wag of its tail, as if to ask what all the racket was about. The dog did not know, but the man did. Paradise was invading Delaney.

CHAPTER THIRTY-THREE

Wolfe heard the crash of a chair falling onto the concrete floor of the abandoned service station as the guard with his shotgun jumped to his feet and ran out into the melee. That was all Wolfe needed in order to make his escape. He had extraordinary strength, it was true, but he was no comic book superhero, and being strong was not the same thing as being bulletproof. A load of buckshot would take him out as readily as it would anyone else.

Now that the guard was gone, Wolfe went to the locked door and smashed the heel of his hand into the door panel just above the doorknob. The door shattered, and he was able to reach through and slide the bolt back.

He paused at the door leading onto the street to take a look around before charging outside. The street was empty. He could see bursts of light coming from behind the houses and few businesses on either side of the main drag. They looked like miniature lightning flashes, but of course, it was gunfire.

One glance and he knew what was happening. Whatever it might have been that Kent Laffrey wanted them to do, the people of Delaney had adopted Wolfe's entrapment plan, after all. They had built barricades across the alley mouths and placed otherwise useless cars and pickup trucks at either extremity of the street, ready to be rolled into place once the Paradise invading force was between them. From the front of the makeshift jail, Wolfe could see the cars and trucks parked, waiting to be positioned. Across the street from him, he could see barricades made of old furniture and who knew what else.

The problem was that the men from Paradise had not come rolling down Main in their wagons. They'd come on foot, creeping close in a wide and circling move, coming in behind the barricades. Wolfe wondered if there had been an alarm given. If the Delaney guards were only posted on the highway east of town, they would have been taken completely unaware. Wolfe suspected that was exactly what had happened. He felt a sense of deep, guilty hopelessness. This was his plan and it was a failure. Instead of trapping the Paradise force, it misdirected the Delaney defenders and allowed them to be overwhelmed by the superior numbers and armament of the people from Paradise.

As suddenly as it had begun, and as vicious as the fighting must have been, the rattle of gunfire was already subsiding from one end of the street to the other. Wolfe felt heartsick over it, but there was nothing he could do, not at this point. His concern now was that he get out of sight. If he were captured, he would surely be executed by a vengeful Mistress Alethia, and that would help no one.

"Go back," Wolfe said to the dog, sweeping his hand in a motion to send the animal back into the service station. The dog obeyed and Wolfe commanded, "Stay," then closed the door to ensure it would not attempt to join him and give him away.

With that, he took a quick look up and down the street to

make sure no one was watching, then took hold of the down spout and climbed hand-over-hand onto the gas station roof. He lay down there behind the business's sign and settled in to wait until he could be reasonably sure of remaining free. Besides, he wanted to be close enough to see what was happening here in town before he decided on his next move.

There were a few final cracks of pistol shots, and then at the east end of Delaney, a red flare rose into the sky and burst like a skyrocket, obviously a prearranged signal to someone. It probably meant that Delaney had been taken, its residents captured. Lord that had been quick. And so very easy. And it was all his fault. The defense plan was his, so now was responsibility for the defeat. Wolfe put his head down and offered up a prayer of heartfelt apology. He could not have been more miserable than at this moment, not even when he had first realized that those flashes of light in the sky meant his beloved country was under nuclear attack by her enemies. Even that had not been as bad, because at least that war was not his fault. The loss of this infinitely smaller war was on Jim Wolfe's conscience, and it weighed very heavy there.

CHAPTER THIRTY-FOUR

Wolfe watched from his rooftop perch as horse-drawn wagons were driven in from where they'd been waiting a mile or more to the east. The residents of Delaney were herded out of their homes into the street, then grouped according to age and sex and loaded into the wagons. There were not enough wagons to carry them all, so the younger, stronger men were held in a bunch at the tail end of the wagon train, surrounded by armed guards.

One young male, looked like a teenage boy, Wolfe thought, panicked and tried to run to safety. One of the guards shot him in the back. Another walked over to stand over the writhing, crying boy, and finished him with a bullet in the head.

The prisoners were silent after that, and there were no further attempts to escape.

Wolfe noticed that the people stood mutely, staring toward the ground for the most part. No one seemed willing to look anyone else in the eyes.

Once the population of Delaney was well under control, squads of Paradise goons fanned out through the town and started going through the buildings one at a time, looking for any holdouts who might be hiding from the invaders. Wolfe guessed they were looking for anything worth looting, also, because one wagon was held back, ready to carry anything of value that could be recovered.

The prisoners were required to wait while a quick initial sweep was made through their town. Then four very large and muscular thugs were left behind with the one empty wagon, while all the others started east toward Paradise. Paradise. Wolfe found the name was foul in his mouth now. Some Paradise.

He saw with surprise that there was one Delaney resident who was exempt from the rough treatment accorded all the others. Kent Laffrey was set out onto the seat of the lead wagon, treated like a hero, which, to Alethia, he might very well be. No wonder Laffrey spoke against Wolfe. The Paradise invaders must have planned an assault that would have been vulnerable to a surprise entrapment on Main Street. That would be why Laffrey opposed it. And when the council decided to set the trap anyway, Laffrey must have gotten word to Alethia that the invasion plan had to be changed at the last minute. Kent Laffrey sold out his own friends and neighbors for...what? Thirty pieces of silver? Or whatever the current equivalent would be, Wolfe judged. Whatever he was promised. Wolfe hoped the SOB choked on it.

Just before the wagons began moving, Wolfe saw Laffrey turn and point toward the old service station where Wolfe now lay hiding on the roof. Was Laffrey selling him out, too? Probably so.

Indeed, one of the Paradise leaders spoke to the cleanup squad who had been busy carrying boxes and bundles out of a derelict movie house, probably Delaney's food storehouse, and they headed at a trot toward the gas station where Wolfe had been imprisoned.

The main body of invaders and their prisoners turned their attention eastward toward Paradise while the cleanup crew came to get Wolfe. Wolfe had no illusions about what they intended to do with him once he was in their hands. Had they wanted him as a prisoner, they would have taken him and put him with the others before the train moved off. Instead, the prisoners were all being taken to Paradise without him. It seemed certain these men intended to kill him here in Delaney and not go to the trouble of hauling him all the way back to Paradise for disposal.

As far as Alethia was concerned, Wolfe's sentence was already passed. The only thing remaining was to execute that sentence and Jim Wolfe.

Wolfe flexed his muscles and rose into a crouch behind the signboard atop the service station. The four bully boys were coming close now; the Paradise wagons were not terribly far away, but no one in the wagons was likely paying much attention to what lay behind. Besides, it was night. Wolfe could see perfectly under these conditions, but the others were literally in the dark and there were no night vision goggles in evidence here. Whatever happened between himself and the Paradise death squad, no one else was likely to interfere.

The four thugs reached the end of the block. Their pace slowed, and they headed past the gasoline pumps toward the door of the Delaney jail.

CHAPTER THIRTY-FIVE

"He's locked in the storage room?" Wolfe heard a voice inquire.

"That's what they said. Him and that dog of his."

"Well, watch out for the dog when you get in. Shoot it first. Then we'll take the guy."

"I don't know about you guys, but I want to take this one alive. You saw what he did to Andrew. I want to make him pay for that."

"He must be pretty tough, Jack. Andrew wouldn't have been any pushover."

"Against four of us? That'll be the day."

"All right then, but shoot the dog first, then we'll swarm the guy. We'll tie him up and everybody have a go at him. Take turn and turn about until he's dead. That way everybody gets to have some fun with him."

Fun, Wolfe thought. So this was what these boys considered to be fun. If he had had any regrets about what he intended to do to them, those thoughts were gone now. These thugs deserved whatever they received. They'd gone to

Paradise to sow the seeds of sin and violence; now it was time for the whirlwind to reap the fruits of those seeds.

Wolfe heard the gas station door being opened and the voices recede indoors. He stepped over the sign and dropped lightly to the ground behind the four men.

CHAPTER THIRTY-SIX

The last of the four was barely inside the door when Wolfe dropped behind him. The man heard Wolfe hit the concrete and spun around. Wolfe landed in a crouch, his knees bent to absorb the impact of the fall, and he came upright in a rush, slamming the heel of his right hand into the fellow's face. The man's head snapped back. Wolfe could hear a crunch as the neck broke, and the would-be murderer crumbled.

For one fleeting instant, Wolfe wondered if this was the one who thought it would be 'fun' for them to take turns killing him, after first killing the dog. Wolfe was as angry about their threat to shoot the dog as he was about their plan to murder him. Damn them anyway.

The man hit the floor with a clatter and the next two in line turned around. Wolfe leaped across the body of their fallen comrade and attacked before they had time to realize what was happening. All four had firearms and he did not want to give them time to bring their weapons into play.

His main advantages were the combination of bewildering speed and vastly superior vision. Here indoors, it would be very dark to the three from Paradise. Wolfe knew he was silhouetted against the night sky outside; he slipped to one side to take that away from them and continued his charge, bolting into one man and flinging him off his feet. Wolfe bent and scooped that man off the floor, lifting him like a bag of feed and throwing him in an underhand motion into the chest of the next one in line. Both men, the one Wolfe threw and then one who was hit by the several hundred pounds of bone and muscle, went sprawling onto the floor.

The one who had been first in line was standing at the storage room door. The lock was already smashed from when Wolfe broke out, so he only needed to pull it open. That's when Wolfe turned the dog loose to race into the station to wreak havoc. The man held his rifle ready to shoot whoever came out of the storage room. Instead, Wolfe came in, fast and furious. The SOB was ready to shoot his dog, and Wolfe was mad.

He knocked the rifle out of the man's hands with a chop across his arms that broke both the thug's forearms. The Paradise goon shrieked in pain and dropped his rifle just in time to receive the dog's charge, the big crossbreed leaping at his throat from inside the blackness of the storage room.

Wolfe left that one to the dog and spun to make sure of the two he'd thrown onto the floor. Those two were getting themselves sorted out and coming to their feet. One of them had recovered his rifle from the floor and was trying to bring it to bear. Before he had time to aim and fire, Wolfe kicked him in the teeth, the sole of Wolfe's shoes breaking the man's jaw.

Wolfe grabbed the gun and twisted it out of his hands, then took it by the barrel and made a backhanded swing as hard as anything Sampras or Agassi ever hit. The stalk of the rifle broke, so did the goon's face.

Behind him, Wolfe could hear the dog snarling and the fading screams of a dying man, leaving only one invader who posed any danger. That one was on his hands and knees, fumbling about on the floor in search of his pistol. Wolfe could see it even if the goon couldn't. It lay several feet away.

Eventually, the fellow probably could have found it; Wolfe didn't give him time to do that. Wolfe stood over him, took the man's head between his hands like a center grabbing a football, and gave it a sharp twist. Again he heard the crunch of bone breaking, and the man went limp in his hands.

Wolfe dropped the body and leaned over his partner to check for signs of life. There were none, so he turned back to see how the dog was doing with his invader. That one would not be shooting anyone again, neither human nor otherwise. He lay in a pool of dark, quickly-spreading blood from a severed carotid artery.

The dog stood there wagging its tail, its tongue lolling out and a happy expression on its furry face.

"Good boy," Wolfe said, patting his thigh to summon the dog closer so he could pet and praise it.

He took a few moments with the dog, giving the four men a cursory glance. Three were dead. The one who had been closest to the door, the first one Wolfe hit, had a broken neck and seemed to have no control of his limbs and probably no feeling below the neck, either, but he was still alive.

Wolfe took him by the shirt and lifted him up to eye level.

"Did you have fun here tonight?" he asked in a soft, controlled whisper. "Is this what you had in mind? Do you really think your friends in Paradise will feed you and clean you and take care of a quadriplegic? Hm? Do you really think they will do that for you now that you're of no use to them? Well, I'll tell you what, bub. I'm going to let you find out. I'm going to leave you here, leave you alive, so you can think about all those things while you're waiting for someone to come and find you."

Wolfe let go of the man's shirt and let him drop onto the concrete floor. The back of his head hit with a loud thump and bounced. If the man was lucky, Wolfe thought, that would finish him off. It didn't, though. Wolfe could still see a shallow rise and fall of the paralyzed man's chest. Good. That would give him time to contemplate his sins.

Wolfe reached down to scratch the dog's ears. He glanced at his rucksack still propped in the corner of the gas station office. It, along with his bow and blowgun, could stay there a little longer. Before he gave thought to moving on, there were a few other things he wanted to do.

He moved through the dark building, collecting rifles and pistols, and the magazines of ammunition to feed them. It was, he thought, a fine night to go hunting.

CHAPTER THIRTY-SEVEN

Following the Paradise caravan turned out to be no problem at all. They had to move slowly because of the Delaney prisoners who were on foot, and Wolfe caught up to them in well under an hour. He walked along the sides of the road, not out onto it, figuring that he would not be seen there in the dark, while he just might be spotted if he was out on the smooth highway surface.

The dog trotted close at his heels, not seeming to mind in the least that its muzzle and chest were caked stiff with the dried blood of the man that the animal killed back in Delaney. The dog might not mind that, but Wolfe reminded himself to wash the animal down the next chance he got. Not too soon, though. There would be more blood flowing before that time was likely to arrive.

Wolfe judged it was some time past midnight when the wagon train stopped—giving the pedestrians a rest, perhaps, or the horses?

The truth turned out to be neither.

The procession had been met by a very handsome carriage coming west out of Paradise. After a few moments,

Mistress Alethia herself stepped daintily out of the carriage and was helped onto the driver's seat a good six feet or more off the ground. She stood in the driving box like a grande dame—a queen surveying her subjects, and the human spoils of war who were now hers also.

Wolfe crept closer, protected by the darkness. Finally, he had a good view. The dog, he noted, dropped to its belly and crawled beside him without him having to tell it to. Not that he would have known how to convey that command even if he'd thought of it. The dog whined a little once Wolfe was in position behind a clump of dry, sunbaked grass where he could not present a solid outline that might be spotted.

"Hush," he whispered.

The dog dropped its chin onto its front paws and lay still, except for the occasional rise and fall of its eyebrows.

Over on the highway, Kent Laffrey was brought before the queen bee. Wolfe wished he were close enough to over-hear what was being said, but it was obvious that Laffrey was being praised. Wolfe wondered what the price of perfidy was in Paradise. Liquor? Women? Whatever it was, Kent Laffrey wanted it bad enough to betray his friends and neighbors in order to possess it.

After the little ceremony, Alethia had the prisoners marched before her in single file. She stopped several of the men, mostly young and fit-looking specimens, and briefly spoke to them. Each responded with a shake of his head and was then permitted to join the others who had already made this passage for Alethia's review.

A half-dozen of the women, two who looked like teenage girls and four older to middle-aged women were returned to the wagons under guard. One woman with graying hair broke away from the others and came to fling herself at Kent Laffrey. At first, Wolfe thought she was attacking him. Instead, she threw her arms around his neck and wept. His wife, perhaps, Wolfe guessed. She was allowed to stay like that for only a moment, then Laffrey gently unwrapped her arms from his neck and spoke to her. Reluctantly, she returned to the crowd of prisoners who had already passed before Alethia.

When Rebecca's turn came, she stood proudly erect, chin high and shoulders firm. Alethia had the girl lifted up to the carriage box and slashed Becca across the face with a backhanded blow hard enough to twist her head to the side and bring blood streaming out of her nose. Alethia said something, and Becca was trussed in rope and tossed into the back of one of the wagons.

The line moved quickly after that. In all, nine women and one man were held aside in the back of a wagon—nine, that is, not counting Rebecca. Finally, Alethia nodded. The guards barked loudly, "Move! Move! Over there!" Loudly enough for Wolfe to easily hear. They prodded the prisoners with the muzzles of their rifles, herding them off the road and out onto the dry, baked earth of the high desert land there.

"Together! Group close together! That's right, now down. Get down on your knees! Anyone who stands up or tries to run will be in big trouble," ordered the guard who seemed to be in charge. Wolfe could not recognize him, but he thought the man's voice sounded vaguely familiar. "Closer! Move in closer! No gaps! You there, and you! Tighten it up! That's right. Shut that kid up, lady! No bawling there. I want quiet!"

Eventually, the head guard had everyone situated the way he wanted them. He nodded. The other guards moved in to form a semicircle around what was virtually the entire population of Delaney. The head guard looked at Alethia, who nodded her approval of the arrangement.

"All right!" the head guard said in a parade ground voice. "Now!"

The muzzles of the M16 automatic rifles came up, and

the guns began to clatter in quick, tearing bursts, sending swarms of small-caliber, high-velocity bullets into the helpless prisoners.

"Oh, Jesus!" Wolfe blurted.

He threw an arm across the dog and held it down. Sixty or seventy yards away, the merciless slaughter went on, and on, and on.

CHAPTER THIRTY-EIGHT

Wolfe lay motionless in the chill night air, stunned by the hammering noise of the automatic weapons and the screams of the dying. There must have been more than a hundred people there. Alethia and her murderers were killing all of them.

Wolfe drew the dog closer to him. It was trembling violently, or so he thought. After a few moments he realized that he was the one who was shaking so badly. The dog whimpered and pressed close to him, but Wolfe did not know if he wished to take comfort from him or give comfort to him.

The sustained rapid-fire petered out and eventually died away. Wolfe heard excited, happy voices and the occasional single shot, as men moving through the seas of bodies paused to dispatch someone who was wounded, but still living.

So many. So very many.

Wolfe felt a momentary impulse to weep for the dead. As quickly as that emotion came to him, though, it was wiped away by a quiet, deadly fury. They had to pay for this crime against all humanity. Alethia had to pay, and he knew of only one person who was able to do that. Possibly able, that is.

He lay where he was, calmer now that he knew what he wanted to do, and watched while the Paradise killers finished their grisly chore and returned to the now lightly-loaded wagons. Of all the people from Delaney, only that handful survived. One young man and nine women.

Wolfe guessed the young girls were destined to serve in Alethia's brothel as rewards for her faithful heroes, while the older women would be taken as slaves and given house-keeping tasks to perform. Plus Rebecca. God knew what Alethia had in mind for Becca's fate. The only thing Wolfe felt reasonably sure of was it would be both ugly and painful. The girl had helped Wolfe escape and several of Alethia's goons died because of that. He was sure the evil woman would not allow Becca's thirst for freedom to go unpunished.

So there were those ten who remained from the assault on Delaney. Those ten, and the much-honored Kent Laffrey. Wolfe wanted to spit just to get the taste of Laffrey's name out of his mouth.

"You bastard," he whispered into the night as the Paradise caravan rolled eastward. "I want you, Laffrey. You and that evil bitch you chose to serve."

He waited for the wagons to continue out of sight, then went to look for a place where he could hole up and sleep through the day. It was late and would too quickly be dawn. He would wait until nightfall again before he made his approach to Paradise, for the night was his ally, and now, there was no longer a reason for him to hurry. The people he wanted to help were nearly all dead.

CHAPTER THIRTY-NINE

Wolfe woke late in the afternoon. There was still enough daylight that he needed the goggles, but the sun would soon be gone. He had spent the day in a fitful, sweltering sleep in the back seat of a wrecked Lincoln that had been stripped of valuables a long time ago. Even the battery and some of the engine parts were missing, which suggested to him that the Paradise people had taken them.

He sat up and looked around, but could not see the dog. Alarmed, he came out of the car in a hurry, only to find the big dog sitting in the late afternoon sunlight with fresh blood on its muzzle and what looked like bits of rabbit fur strewn about on the ground.

"Been hunting, boy?"

The dog wagged its tail.

"Well, we're gonna do some more of it pretty soon."

The dog seemed to have taken care of its own supper. Wolfe was hungry now, too, and even more thirsty. Those things could wait, though.

He picked up the pair of rifles he'd taken from the dead men back in Delaney, and checked the pistol shoved in the hip pocket of his jeans. He also had a nylon backpack of the sort schoolchildren used to carry, back when there were schools and a normal, civilized way of life. The bag was supposed to hold books and pencils and love notes passed among teenagers; now, it was heavy with the magazines of .223 cartridges he'd collected from the dead.

He slung the spare M16 over his shoulder and carried the other ready in his hands. There might well be guards posted along the highway to intercept anyone the murderers might have missed back in Delaney. As a precaution against that, Wolfe moved a half-mile south of the highway before he turned east.

Then he began to jog, moving at a steady pace that would quickly eat up the few remaining miles to Paradise. The dog trotted at his side with an easy, fluid gait that it could probably maintain for hours on end. If he timed it right, Wolfe thought, he should reach Mistress Alethia's wicked burg just about the time full night fell. For Jim Wolfe, that should be just about right.

CHAPTER FORTY

Paradise had electricity, but it was not wired into the streetlights that still lined the roads, so Wolfe had no trouble moving into the town and slipping, unseen, through its alleys. He knew good and well that one man—well, one man and a dog—cannot take on a small army of armed foes and expect to accomplish very much other than his own demise. And he was really not particularly interested in dying. Instead of trying to fight them all, he narrowed his goals to finding—and in somewhat different ways, taking care of—three particular people.

Rebecca was his first priority, he decided; he owed her that. She had been brave and very helpful. She'd trusted him. Now, she was back in the hands of Mistress Alethia and the woman's thugs. Wolfe intended to find Becca and take her out of harm's way once and for all.

Next on his list would have to be Alethia herself. She was evil in the oldest, truest sense of the word, he believed. She did not have the excuse of madness; Alethia was very simply a vile, evil person, and she had to be stopped.

More, she had to be destroyed. Wolfe had no intention of

staying here to supervise Alethia's future behavior, and there was no competent legal authority capable of imprisoning or otherwise punishing her. For Alethia, the answer of necessity would be harsh and must take no account of the fact that she was a woman. Women can be as evil as anyone, and Alethia was much worse than anyone Wolfe had ever encountered before. Alethia, in short, had to die.

That was the only way this cult of violence could be smashed forever. The leader had to be eliminated. What was that old saying? 'Cut off the head, and the body will die'? It is a truism that applies equally to snakes and cults, Wolfe believed. It was his intention now to cut this snake's head off.

And finally, third and last in his order of priority, there was Kent Laffrey. The man betrayed the neighbors and friends who trusted him and placed him on their governing council. And then, having played Judas to his neighbors, he deliberately sent his own wife into that field to die with all the others. Laffrey, too, deserved to feel the sting of retribution's lash. Wolfe intended to be the one to apply it. Silently, he and the dog moved into the town of Paradise.

CHAPTER FORTY-ONE

Rebecca first, he told himself. If nothing and no one else, he had to take care of Rebecca first. The only place he knew to look for her was the old motel that Alethia used as a brothel to reward her faithful subjects. Becca was young and she was pretty, and she hated the humiliation of being forced to serve as a prostitute slave. Wolfe thought it entirely possible that she would suffer physical punishment now that she had been captured again, and then be returned to the sordid duties that she'd had to perform before.

He made his way through the town to the outskirts where light showed business being conducted as usual at the motel. But, of course, now there were many heroes whose exploits had to be rewarded by the leader. How many men of Paradise earned praise and honor by slaughtering the help- less captives from Delaney? Wolfe was sure Alethia would have put extra slaves to work just to take care of all those deserving heroes. Thinking about that put a scowl on Wolfe's face and made his mood bitter as he approached the back of the motel.

Light showed in all the rooms, so he started at one end

and worked his way toward the other, slipping quietly through the night and peeping into windows like a common criminal.

The second room from the end was occupied by a girl he was sure he recognized from Delaney, already being pressed into service here. She was bleeding and her face streaked with tears. There were three Paradise men in the room with her; Wolfe guessed the idea was to so debase and humiliate her that her will would be broken, and she would offer no resistance in the future, regardless of what might be required of her.

Wolfe was sorely tempted to break in and end the horror, but he dared not do that. None of the three appeared to be armed and Wolfe knew he could overpower them easily, but he could not do so instantly. There would be time for any of them to raise an outcry, and if they did that, Wolfe would become the hunted. He would have to hide from the armed warriors of Paradise and that would make it difficult, perhaps impossible, for him to carry out the things that he had to do here tonight.

He felt terrible for the girl and felt all the worse that he was leaving her to the mercies of three men who had no mercy, but he simply had no choice about it. He had to move along.

The fourth window he looked into gave him a surprise. Kent Laffrey was inside the room. He had two girls with him and a bottle of wine. Kent seemed to be thoroughly enjoying his reward. Wolfe made a note of which room Laffrey was occupying, then continued down the line in search of Becca. Rebecca had to come first. Regardless of Wolfe's own personal feelings, Becca was at the top of his priority list.

Except Rebecca was not in any of the motel rooms. Wolfe even looked inside the office where a heavyset young man had replaced the recently departed Andrew as manager of the establishment. Becca was nowhere to be seen.

Wolfe paused in the deep shadows at the back of the motel to consider. Should he leave Laffrey there while he went on looking, or should he take care of Kent now and then continue his search?

At the time, Wolfe happened to be standing close to the room where the innocent girl from Delaney was being introduced to the ugliness of her fate. Laffrey was responsible for that. The man was responsible for so very many deaths, so much pain, and now for this. There was no reason, Wolfe thought, why he should not take this opportunity to administer a little homemade justice to Mr. Laffrey now that he happened to be in the neighborhood. But quietly. Quietly.

Wolfe set the rifles and backpack full of ammunition down in the shadows, and motioned for the dog to stay on guard with them. Then he silently went around to the front of the motel and counted the rooms to make sure he had the right one. Waiting would only make it all the more likely that someone could come along and see him there before Wolfe wanted to be seen.

Without hesitation, he stepped to the motel room door, took hold of the knob, and twisted it until he heard the crunch that told him the lock broke. He pushed the door open and stepped inside.

CHAPTER FORTY-TWO

"Oh, God!"

"Nope," Wolfe said quietly. "It's just me. God will see you in a few minutes, though, I think."

"But, they told me…Th-they said--"

"That I'm dead?" Wolfe asked. He shook his head. "They were wrong, Kent. I have to tell you something, though. You weren't wrong when you advised the good folks back home that they shouldn't set that trap along Main Street. No, sir, you were right on the money about that. They went and did it anyway and look what happened. They lost. Imagine that! Why, it's almost as if Alethia's people knew what the plan was so they could adjust their plans accordingly. Don't you think it looked like that, Kent? How do you think a thing like that could've happened, anyway?"

Wolfe laid a finger over his lips and smiled and motioned for Laffrey's two girls to step into the bathroom. The girls looked frightened, but there was no telling what, if anything, they might have been told about this white-haired madman who came among them like an avenging whirlwind. The two of them jumped off the bed and scampered out of sight, pulling the bathroom door shut behind them. Wolfe heard the click of a lock being set.

"Looks like we're alone, Kent," he said.

"I-I didn't—look, mister, M-Mr. Wolfe, I can explain! It isn't what you think! I can explain, really I can!"

"I believe you, Kent. I really do. Didn't I just say how right you were about the plan to defend Delaney? Doesn't that prove how smart you are? How successful? I believe everything you tell me, Kent. I'm just like Lieutenant Columbo that way."

"Oh, Jesus!" Laffrey moaned. Wolfe could see a stain spreading across the bedding as Laffrey's terror caused him to wet himself.

Wolfe reached down and took hold of the man, wrapped his fingers around Laffrey's throat, and looked into the trembling man's eyes.

"Don't!" Laffrey whispered. "Please don't!"

"It is not my place to judge you, Kent Laffrey," Wolfe said softly. "But I will send you before the one who will judge you and all you've done."

"I'll tell you-tell you anything! A-anything!"

"Anything?" Wolfe asked.

Laffrey shook his head vigorously. "Please?" He began to cry.

"Where is Rebecca Morrison?"

"Who?"

"The girl from Tifton who escaped with me. I saw them tie her and throw her into one of the wagons. She wasn't murdered along with the others whose blood is on your hands. Where is Rebecca now?"

"M-Mistress Alethia, she took the girl, she has her now… had her the last I knew, anyway!"

"Thank you."

"You'll let me go now? You really will?" Laffrey begged.

"No. I really won't," Wolfe said.

His hand contracted like a steel vice, inexorably clamping tightly shut. Laffrey made a faint, muted gurgling sound and went limp.

Wolfe did not know if Laffrey was faking or not, so he resolved the question by giving his wrist a quick twist, snapping the man's neck. There would be no faking now.

CHAPTER FORTY-THREE

Wolfe thought about the girls who were hiding in the bathroom. They were capable of giving an alarm, but there was only one sure way to eliminate that possibility. It was a method he would never in good conscience be able to employ. No way could he kill them, for they were as innocent as those poor people of Delaney had been. The girls were victims, not acolytes, and Wolfe could never bring himself to harm them.

He could tie them up, but that might only anger them, and they still could free themselves or at least manage to make noise to attract attention from people in nearby rooms.

In the end, he did nothing, nor did he say anything to them. With luck, they would remain in the bathroom hiding. Without luck, he would just have to take his chances. He turned the light off and removed his goggles, then listened at the door for a moment before stepping outside.

The street was deserted, though he could hear sounds of merriment from somewhere in the next block. Music. But, of course, Paradise had music. Car stereos operated on twelve volts of power, playing the CDs or cassette tapes that were manufactured before the war—if things had been different, but they were not, were they? Paradise, as Alethia constructed it, was an evil place. Sodom and Gomorrah reincarnate and no Paradise at all.

Still, what Alethia's followers did here, James Wolfe could duplicate somewhere else. All he needed to do was to find Lurleen and Jojo. Then he, too, could seek out a windmill to spin a belt-driven generator, hook up a few twelve volt lights and a stereo. Oh, my! He could have music again when that day came.

In the meantime, however, there were things he still had to do here in the town that used to be Tifton.

He gave a look up and down the street and went around to the back of the motel to retrieve his rifles and ammunition, then started off toward the town square. He did not know where Alethia's private quarters were, but the courthouse where he had first seen the redhead would be as good a starting point as any.

He kept to the shadows, the dog trotting closely behind, and he crossed the town without being spotted. The imposing granite face of the courthouse was dark. Wolfe circled around it. There. Lights blazed from four ceiling-high windows on the third floor, and again, he could hear music.

Back near the motel, the sounds had been of country music. This, incongruously, was Sinatra crooning into the night. Alethia's taste? It would not surprise him.

He went back around to the front of the massive courthouse and stood for several minutes, waiting to see if any guards had been posted. If there were, they were being very patient and very still. Wolfe knew he was not going to accomplish anything by standing here waiting to be discovered by some passerby. He took one more slow and searching look all around, then started up the stone steps to the courthouse doors.

CHAPTER FORTY-FOUR

There was a guard, but he had been in the men's room. Wolfe heard the faint sound of a toilet flushing, and a moment later, saw the thread of light under the bathroom door disappear. The door opened and an armed guard stepped out. He was yawning and carried his M16 slung casually over his shoulder.

The guard's eyes went wide when he saw Wolfe coming toward him in the gloom. His mouth opened to shout an alarm, but Wolfe did not give him time. Wolfe chopped the man's throat with the hard edge of his hand, crushing the guard's windpipe and silencing him, except for the futile drumming of the man's heels on the marble floor, and the wet sound of his death rattle a moment later.

Wolfe took the man by the collar, not waiting for him to finish the important business of dying, and dragged him inside the men's room. As a final precaution, he stripped the rifle off the guard's shoulder and slid it across the floor beneath the door to the nearest stall.

Wolfe poked his head out to make sure there was no one else on duty in the lobby, then took the stairs in a rush. When he got there, Sinatra had been replaced by an instrumental recording. Percy Faith, he thought, although he would not have sworn to that.

Whoever the artist, the sound guided Wolfe down a long corridor to the back of the building. He guessed this area would have been reserved for the office suites occupied by the judges. The thought probably appealed to Alethia now that she had set herself up as the judge of all she surveyed, complete with the powers of life and death. Well, she'd had her chance to dispense life, had she chosen to do so. Now it would be her turn to experience death.

The door to Alethia's quarters was not locked, but then who, after all, would dare intrude on the leader without her consent? Wolfe paused to pull the welding goggles over his eyes—it would not do to let himself be blinded when he went in—then opened the door and stepped inside.

He stopped dead still once he saw what lay beyond the heavy oak doors. He saw, and he gagged, his gorge rising in his throat. He tried to fight it back, then gave up and spewed the meager contents of his stomach onto the thick carpet in Alethia's private rooms.

Never had he seen, never had he imagined anything so terrible as this.

CHAPTER FORTY-FIVE

B ecca. Poor Becca.

Wolfe could not imagine the suffering Rebecca had to endure before death brought her a measure of peace at last.

Rebecca had been stripped naked, and Alethia was naked as well, save for the blood and gore that had splattered onto her, and which now painted much of her lower body a dull red.

Alethia looked pleased with herself, still haughty. Seated as if on a throne, although this throne was no more than a chair upholstered in gold brocade. Still, she acted very much the queen whose subjects had better obey if they knew what was good for them, acted as if her throne was indeed gold and not mere cloth. The only problem with her imperious attitude was that Jim Wolfe was not one of her subjects, and none of her guards was close by now.

Wolfe regained control of himself and, avoiding looking at Becca again, strode purposefully across the room to stand before the devilishly beautiful redhead.

"Mind your place," Alethia ordered. "My men will kill you if I wish it."

"I don't think so," Wolfe said.

"Come no closer, or I shall scream."

"Why is it that I think there's been a whole lot of screaming in here today? I doubt a little more will draw any attention."

"I can kill you myself," Alethia threatened. "I will do it. I will do to you what I did to her, and I will enjoy it, just as I enjoyed doing this to her."

She pointed, but Wolfe's eyes did not follow the sweep of Alethia's hand. He saw, therefore, when her hand slipped between her chair's cushions and emerged with a long, slender dagger.

Wolfe slapped the knife from her fingers, sending it spinning across the room to bang against the handsome wall paneling and fall harmlessly to the floor.

"You hurt me!" Alethia complained.

"No, not yet. But I intend to."

Alethia screamed, again and again, and on for what seemed a very long time. And Wolfe was right. None of Alethia's men responded to her cries. Not a single one of them thought there was anything at all unusual about the sound of pain and terror emanating from that chamber of horrors.

Eventually, as disgusted with himself as he was with her, Wolfe finished what had to be done and walked away. He wanted to go home now. Home to decency and kindness. Home to family and love.

"Come on, boy. We have a long way still to travel, you and me."

The dog trotted faithfully at his heels as he made his way out into the night, and hurried away from this false Paradise.

ABOUT THE AUTHOR

Frank Roderus wrote his first story—it was a western—when he was five. It was really awful, as might be expected, but his mother kept that typed and spell-checked short story tucked away until the day she died.

Later, Frank became a newspaper reporter, thinking that books are written by authors which he most assuredly was not. He kept trying to write though, and eventually did it wrong enough to learn how to get it right. That first sale, a young adult novel published by Independence Press, was more than thirty years and a good many books ago.

As a journalist, the Colorado Press Association awarded Frank Roderus their highest award, the Sweepstakes Award, for the best news story of 1980, and the Western Writers of America has twice named Frank recipient of their prestigious Spur Award.

Frank passed away at age 73 in December 2015.

NOTES - CRAIG MARTELLE

WRITTEN APRIL 17, 2019

Thank you for reading this far! You have my sincere appreciation for sticking with us and reading our stories.

You are here because you read the first Nightwalker and thought it was good enough to read the second and now the third!

You are on board and that means you are my favorite reader! I will strive to tell every story better than the last. Keep you guessing and following along as the world changes and Jim Wolfe changes with it. What will his soul look like when he reaches Florida? I hope it is the soul of Easter that a new day will rise, regardless of what he finds.

I have four more stories in mind should we want to follow Jim Wolfe on his trek home. I think we should. There's a lot of great things a man will see when he's walking across America, or what used to be America.

Frank Roderus passed away in 2015 but he lives in every word he wrote. You get a glimpse of the man in each of these stories as Frank put himself there, in a world torn apart by war, divided by those who have power, suffered by those without. I hope that I've done Frank justice with my touch ups on these stories. If you can't tell the difference, then I have done my job in helping make these good post-apoc tales for the 21st Century.

Spring has come early to my neck of the woods. It snowed a little last night, but that will melt today and we'll be back in the 50s by the weekend. This close to the Arctic, we always expect it to be cold. When it's not, those are bonus days. The northernmost golf course in North America is only a few miles from my house. I think they might open early, like mid-May early. I need to get out this year. I hit balls once last year and didn't play a single round. I used to play three days a week. But then again, I never expected to retire to a place where the golf courses are open only three to four months out of the year.

But, my wife is a professor and this is where she is in her tenure track position. I can work from anywhere and do. I write while I travel. We go to places where she's on vacation, but I'm working. I write, I publish, and I market, then do it all again the next day. But this is the best gig I've ever had.

I hope you enjoy the stories. It's been a long time in bringing them to you, but now that they have built their foundation, they will continue. Thank you for coming along on this great ride with me.

Have a great day.

BOOKS BY CRAIG MARTELLE

Craig Martelle's other books (listed by series)

Terry Henry Walton Chronicles (co-written with Michael Anderle) – a post-apocalyptic paranormal adventure

Gateway to the Universe (co-written with Justin Sloan & Michael Anderle) – this book transitions the characters from the Terry Henry Walton Chronicles to The Bad Company

The Bad Company (co-written with Michael Anderle) – a military science fiction space opera

End Times Alaska (also available in audio) – a Permuted Press publication – a post-apocalyptic survivalist adventure

The Free Trader – a Young Adult Science Fiction Action Adventure

Cygnus Space Opera – A Young Adult Space Opera (set in the Free Trader universe)

Darklanding (co-written with Scott Moon) – a Space Western

Rick Banik – Spy & Terrorism Action Adventure

Become a Successful Indie Author – a non-fiction work

Enemy of my Enemy (co-written with Tim Marquitz) – a galactic alien military space opera

Superdreadnought (co-written with Tim Marquitz) – a military space opera

Metal Legion (co-written with Caleb Wachter) - a military space opera

End Days (co-written with E.E. Isherwood) – a post-apocalyptic adventure

Mystically Engineered (co-written with Valerie Emerson) – dragons in space

Monster Case Files (co-written with Kathryn Hearst) – a young-adult cozy mystery series

For a complete list of books from Craig, please see www.craigmartelle.com